What are you supposed to do once you realize there's a danger magnet permanently sewn to your caboose?

Start charging, of course.

2nd Edition

*F*REELANCER

A Freelancer, Inc. Thriller (Case 1.0)

Jeremy Jaynes

Phoenix One Media, LLC
Indianapolis, IN

MEDIA

MEDIA

More information regarding books published by
Phoenix One Media may be obtained from:
www.PhoenixOneAlpha.com

FREELANCER
Second Edition
Phoenix One Media LLC
May 2012

Library of Congress Control Number: 2012908483

For Shelley

Chapter 1
Club Girls, Rich Guys, and Techno
(AKA: I'm in Hell)

When you're six years old and your first elementary school burns to the ground, it's unfortunate.

When you're nine years old and your second elementary school burns down, it's considered odd.

When you're twelve years old and your third school burns down, well, either you're a pyro, or trouble is hunting you down.

In other words, you're me.

The trouble part, not the pyro... but you got that, right?

And I know what you're thinking. It's all some big coincidence. Well, you see, the problem is it doesn't stop there. You know how kids aren't supposed to talk to strangers with candy? I've had six instances of deviants trying to coax me into one ill-advised situation or another. SIX! And sure, you could say maybe I was a looker growing up (thank you), but I don't think so. I mean, I'm not ugly as far as I'm concerned, and I've been told I'm pretty, but I figure those are just people being nice or guys trying to get into my pants.

Regardless, in my book, it had nothing to do with sexy-schoolgirl-syndrome.

I know. I know. I'm being melodramatic and it's all in my head.

Hold that thought.

To date, I've also been in twelve car accidents (only one my fault), four bank robberies, three convenience store holdups, a mall-Santa attack (don't ask), three house fires, one house explosion (my friends' parents put a stop to sleepovers after that), two hurricanes (I live on the west coast), three tornadoes (see: live on the west coast), a riot (our team did win, so I'm not sure if this one counts), the swimming pool I normally go to had a live power line blown into it (everyone survived), a subway train derailment, and don't even get me started on the big stuff. Oh, and the earthquakes... however, I live in California so I don't count those. But the lightning...you wouldn't believe the lightning strikes I've witnessed.

1

Now, after all this, why don't I lock myself in a padded room to protect society from my obvious dangers? Because, after many, many years of this, I realized I wasn't the cause. I'm like some blind hound dog unconsciously sniffing out danger and wandering right up to it for a pat on the head.

Case and point: Those banks and convenience stores – I only shopped regularly at one of them; and those fires/explosions I mentioned – those would have happened with or without me. They were due to faulty electrical lines or gas mains. Even if I had never met my Bad Penny – my best friend since forever – her house still would have burned down. But since I knew her, of course I had to be there when it did. Fate, karma, Zeus – whoever is pulling the strings seems to think I'm the person who needs to be in the wrong place at the right time.

Mom got so worried she began picking up and moving us on an annual basis. And why on Earth she thought staying in New Los Angeles was a good idea, the one city whose penchant for attracting trouble nearly demolished it and turned it into an island, is beyond me. Not kidding! Everyone joked L.A. would eventually fall into the ocean. Well, not that funny when it almost happened.

Actually, it didn't fall off so much as a quake literally opened up what is now the Angelino Bay. The technical people can explain how this happened. All I know is one day there was an earthquake, and the next there's a mile wide bay (I call it a river, but what do I know) separating L.A. from the mainland.

Anyway, so what does one do with her life when she can't exactly sit through a college lecture without fear of the building crumbling around her just because she's sitting in it? She makes it a profession of course.

My name is Elizabeth Freeman, and I'm a Freelancer.

(I feel like I just announced I'm an alcoholic or something…)

A Freelancer, in this case, is a person who takes odd "security" jobs. Some weeks I'm playing bodyguard to the rich, other weeks I might be tracking down and stealing back someone's family heirloom, and others I'm playing cat and mouse with a psycho stalker.

Speaking of, this virgin daiquiri I've been stirring for the past twenty minutes tastes like embalming fluid. There's a funny story on how I know what that tastes like, but I'd rather not relive that memory, thanks. Oh, and P.S., I've got a little over two years before I'm old enough to drink, so, you know, NOT an alchy... or a pyro... making these points clear up front.

"Blood analysis came back empty from the cops," Penny says over my earpiece. The miniscule device is attached to my fake diamond earrings to not be conspicuous. I can attach it to pretty much any type I wear. Being such a handy tool, I rarely leave home without it these days. "Our boy – and they did confirm it's a boy – is obviously not known for troublemaking."

As you can see, at this moment, I need to focus on pretending I'm just another bar girl trolling for a rich mate. Actually, I kind of made myself look like the off-putting bar girl, but that's just part of my well-calculated and slightly flattering ensemble. You've got to understand, the slinky, crimson cocktail dress, dark jeweled necklace, "saucy virgin" red lipstick (do I seriously own a lipstick called "saucy virgin"?), and slightly mussed jet-black, cropped hair (with a slight hint of the purple dye that didn't wash out after last week's job) is probably the most planned part of my cover.

The hair is what I consider key. When my client decided to go out this evening, we both went to her stylist beforehand. Actually, I'm not even sure why this girl wants to go out. If some psycho was snapping photos of me sleeping and sending me vials of blood, there's no way I would go... no, wait. I would totally go out. In fact, I'd probably do my best to goad him into coming after me. But just because I would do it doesn't mean everyone should.

Regardless, I told her stylist the persona I was going for this evening, so she gave me what she called a "jagged muss" cut. My hair is cut into several layers, with specific strands cut into finely sharpened points - the longest of which reach just past my face. The stylist went so far as to leave the hint of purple dye. She said it was only noticeable when light reflected off my locks and added to the image. It's wild, hip, and somewhat dangerous. It's perfect. I can't look approachable because then I'm fending off boys all night. And I can't look too unavailable or I look like I don't belong. In a club like this – whose patrons come from money and are each hoping to settle some score with daddy – I just look like the spoiled rich girl venting her angst through her wardrobe.

3

Please.

I swear, everyone in here is a walking cliché, including my client for the evening – the blonde proceeding to shake her groove thing on the dance floor to the techno beats. Coincidentally, her groove thing's about to show in that short skirt if she's not... oh, I think there it was... She's the most cliché rebelling rich girl I've ever seen. Sixteen years old, meaning she's not even old enough to be in here but still rich enough to get in, a prodigy who just graduated from private school, and stunningly gorgeous, you'd think she has nothing to rebel against.

Worse yet, I'm a little annoyed at myself for being slightly jealous.

Katie Worthington, little miss popular with all the boys flocking to her, has one thing I don't. No, not money... although, I could use more. And, no, it's not smarts or looks. She's pretty, but I think I hold my own. No, it's the carefree way she looks at the world. Up there, dancing like some little trollop, she could care less what anyone thinks of her – something I can't seem to get past.

And I do not get it. I'm the girl that changes her hair and wardrobe on a client by client basis (bar slut this week, debutant next, whatever), so how I feel self-conscious is... I'd say it's "beyond me" but it's not. When I'm on a job, I'm in a costume playing my part. These aren't my clothes and this isn't my hair. So, when I'm not on a case, and I don't have a part to play, I start to wonder who I'm supposed to be. Somehow, Lizzy Freeman gets lost in the shuffle and I become this made up persona.

"So far," Penny calls again, "Security hasn't found a single suspect. Well, none fitting what we're looking for tonight, but considering most come through the back door since they're rich... I'm not helping am I?" My Bad Penny, the girl who seemed to turn up at every other rough situation in high school, was sitting at home in her PJs while running the operation. I envy her.

"Hey there, beautiful," the random rich-boy with a flipped up collar says to me as he pulls up to my cocktail table. "Can I buy you a drink?"

FREELANCER

Ugh, mental note: Don't lean against a table while you're in a short skirt. It's like chumming the water for sharks. This entire time I've been doing so well. I stayed at the table and away from the bar (where many of the sharks circle). I've kept my focus on Katie and on anyone who might be focused on her – which the way she's dancing is everyone at this point – and I've been holding my bladder for half an hour, waiting for when she finally goes to the bathroom. A perfect evening of hiding in plain sight blown because this guy likes my ass.

"Free," a confident voice in my earpiece says, "I've got nothin'. You need me to distract Mr. Perfect or are you two about to set a date already?"

I do my best to maintain eye contact with the rich kid hitting on me, while I slip a hand around my back and flip my middle finger at the terrace above. My friend on the other line is Detective Thomas Dustings, or "Dust" for short. Dust was a rookie on the force, about my current age, when he met a cute little twelve year-old girl with a knack for finding trouble. When he kept noticing this same girl showing up in the middle of crime scenes, he eventually took a protective interest in her. I'm not completely convinced he didn't, at one time, think I was behind all the danger surrounding me. But I don't think it took him very long to figure out it's just my nature. Tonight though, Dust is off duty and Freelancing for me. Believe me when I say having him around makes my job seem a lot easier.

I can hear his snicker through the earpiece. Dust is about as classy as they come and a real gentleman to boot, but he's still male and loves to tease. Penny has the biggest crush on him, and I can't blame her. Tall, dark, handsome and – I'm not kidding when I say this – I have no idea what ethnicity he is. Hey, don't judge. I'm very open minded and don't care about that sort of thing. Just talk to the guy once about his heritage and you'll understand why I bring it up.

Every time I hear about a new relative I find out they are another nationality/race/ethnicity/species/what-have-you. Since he is a melting pot of everything I call him the American Dream.

Ew, I just realized he might think I'm hitting on me when I say that.

5

Wait, back to Lord Money in front of me. Did I hear him say something about "stole the stars from the sky" or just imagine it? Doing my best not to look at him cross-eyed, I notice over the flirty young man's shoulder a figure sitting in a booth across the room. This person's clung to the shadows most of the evening, only throwing Katie an occasional glance from what I can tell. Whoever it is has made it incredibly difficult to be certain where he's looking or even who he is. It's as if he picked the best booth in the house to stalk someone from. Hardly anyone would get close enough to identify you, and barely noticeable if your deviant's stare undresses the girl on the dance floor (not that she has much to take off). And, while Katie might have insulted me when we first met tonight, saying my outfit is "sooo retro" and "sooo two-thousand twenty," I don't want her to get hurt, well, unless it's by me. Then, that's okay.

What? I like this expensive, slutty dress. It's boddin' cool.

Regardless, I was hired due to my unique ability to draw out the crazies, and tonight, her stalker – the guy who sent her a vial of his own blood recently – might just be sitting in that corner.

"I'm sorry, Bill was it?" I finally say to the walking money clip.

"Uh, Charles, actually," he says to the girl who does not care.

"I see a friend," I reply, barely acknowledging his existence. "You'll have to excuse me." I hastily make my retreat from the table, gathering my purse as I do.

"Got something?" Dust asks in my ear.

"Maybe," I mumble. "I'll let you know. Sit tight."

I slink through the crowd, trying to keep as inconspicuous as possible. Luckily, or possibly just as he planned, the shadowy figure's table is on the way to the restroom and the exit beyond, making any movement toward him seem plausible. Oh and how I'd love to just pass him by and relieve my bladder.

FREELANCER

As I close on the table, the crowd gets thicker. The bar is close by and a long, chaotic line has formed. I try to squeeze between a wobbly frat boy whose every other word slurs into some new unintelligible language, and a young man in a fine silver suit and tie. In a place like this, business dress is not uncommon, but I can't help note his surveying gaze as I near him. Nowhere else to go, I squeeze between a drunkard and a young businessman, hoping I can get past. Of course, being a lady, you have to choose: Rub your ass against the suit's ass while you squeeze through, leaving your boobs to rub against the drunky, or put your chest against the suit's back and rub your butt against Mr. Wobblesome. And, for all those keeping score, there is no right answer. As I squeeze past, my derrière turned the drunk's direction, I feel the inebriated young man "accidentally" run his hand across the small of my back and then not-at-all-accidentally cup my right cheek. Ticked off to no end and mortified beyond words, it's taking everything I've got to keep myself from spinning around and cracking him across the skull with the collapsible rod I carry in my purse. I call it my "Mercy stick."

It's irony. Get it?

Instead, I grit my teeth and just keep going. Though, I have made a mental note to "thank" him if I ever get the chance later. Upon reaching the unlit table, I am overly troubled. My prey has vanished. The line to the bar all but ended on the hiding man's doorstep, and I'd barely taken my eyes off him.

"Looking for me, Ms. Freeman," a man too suave for his own good says in a wispy Scottish brogue.

I keep telling myself the tingle I feel when I hear his voice is my sense of danger. It is not at all due to the fact that he's six feet tall, carries a gentleman's gate, serviceman hands, and a bedeviling smile. And, while in his mid thirties, the cut of his suit also tells me he could probably lift an ox.

"Mr. Ketchum," I say, pretending I knew it was him all along. "So, what is my least favorite shadow doing watching my client?"

Ketchum – I still don't have his first name – has a habit of appearing at my more sensitive jobs. He's never gotten in the way and tends to pass on relevant information every time I see him, so he's made it extremely difficult to trust or distrust him. He just... is.

The finely cut man circles so close I can nearly feel his dark stubble against my cheek. He retakes his seat in the booth and scoops up his lonely scotch. As usual, he just wants to prove he can slip past me.

"Oh, I'm just taking in the sites," Ketchum says in a slightly suggestive manner. "And my, they are a wonder to behold this evening. You look rather lovely tonight, Ms. Freeman. I must send a *'thank you'* card to your tailor."

Dust had tried to run a search on Ketchum in the station's computers but was met with a big fat "Access Denied." My brain tries to warn me about him. My naughty bits are, well, not as warning.

"Alright," I return with a folding of my arms, "At this point, I'm guessing you're either some sort of super-spy, or I've got my very own stalker. Maybe even both — a super-stalker. And, you know what, that's one too many stalkers for me tonight."

I'm only half joking.

"Right," Ketchum returns before sipping his drink. "Ms. Worthington's overly-friendly fan, so how's that going?"

"Swell," I reply, unsurprised he somehow knows. "She's having the time of her life."

"Really?" Ketchum says with a slightly sarcastic twist. "Have you asked her lately?"

Poodle on a Pole! I got so caught up listening to William Wallace here that I took my eye off the client. Twisting around, I turn my attention back to the dance floor. Lo and behold, Katie is gone. I turn round and round, cataloging every face in the club. Still I find nothing. As I go to click my earpiece, to call for help — including Dust, Katie's personal Security, and anyone with a can of mace — Ketchum grabs my arm and rises from the booth.

"No need for that, now," he advises. "We need to make sure you still get paid." He nods across the bar to the exit behind the stage. "Backdoor, my dear."

Normally, this is when I'd call the cavalry. But two things are stopping me. One: Ketchum is right. I won't get paid if Katie's security team does my job. But typically, I wouldn't let that stop me. My client's well-being is far more important than folding greens. Number two, however, I really want to see Ketchum in action, and this almost guarantees it.

8

FREELANCER

As we race across the dance floor, likely alerting every private security person in the room (not just our team in a club like this), I notice the drunk who copped a feel wandering right into my path. Four glasses in his hands and one plastic cup charmingly held by the rim in his teeth, I can't help but "accidentally" smack the bottom of one of the glasses as we dart by. I cause what can only be described as a chain reaction of alcoholic tumbling. Each drink crashes into the young man's chest, showering his torso in wasted alcohol before the glasses crash to floor. Unable to resist, I blow him a kiss as I exit out the backdoor, which Ketchum happens to be holding open like a perfect gentleman.

I can't say I'm proud of myself, but the payback is really fulfilling.

Burning through the backdoor, my Mercy-stick is in hand and ready to go. The back of the building is fairly typical of any bar. There's a single road before us, wet from an earlier rain. The ground glows with the eerie, bluish light from the LED streetlamp above. Across the street is a tall, razor wire fence leading to a vacant lot. My first thought is the perp took Katie there, but I realize it would be awfully difficult for him to carry her over a fence that high and with razor wire to boot. Quickly surveying one end of the alley, I find only a green recycling container, a few scattered trash bags, and steam from the club's kitchen wafting across the road. Looking to the other end of the alley, I find even less.

Seeing no sign of Katie, I whisper to Ketchum, "See her?"

Continuing my survey, I find it odd when he doesn't answer. Glancing over my shoulder, I realize something that unnerves me to no end.

I'm alone.

Damn it to hell! I can't even be certain the damned Scot followed me out here. Wanted to make sure I got paid... that ass. I didn't even get it until now. He wasn't coming out here to help me. He was just pointing me in the right direction.

"Dust," I whisper, trying to sound more professional than nervous.

"Already on my way!" he calls into my earpiece. "Please tell me you registered for a gun like I asked you to."

"Umm," I utter in a barely audible reply, "I filled out the paperwork... but I didn't have a stamp."

"Damn it, Free," my friend chastises like the older brother he thinks he is. "You cannot Freelance without a gun."

"Dust," Penny calls, saving me from more of his ire. "Go out the front! I'm not sure how, but Ketchum used an exit that's alarmed. That goes off and the perp might kill Katie. I could crack the alarm code, but it would take too long."

A loud metallic clang echoes from the side of the building, signaling as if Katie's cry for help. The sound is followed by the faint scuffling of feet. I know Dust will be here soon, but I can't wait. Katie might not have that long. I dart down the dark, wet alley, toward the sound in the hopes I'll find my client. One foot after the other – the uncomfortable shooting pain in my heels reminds me six inch stilettos, while they look awesome, are always a bad idea.

Rounding the corner, expecting to see my girl struggling with some crazed ten foot maniac, I instead come face to face with a dagger roughly the size of my Mercy-stick. The blade's ivory sheen – while odd – is barely a footnote considering the tip is nearing my eye. Part luck, part reflex, I rear my head back and duck below the knife. The wind from my assailant's thrust brushes through my hair and I twirl so his fine silver suit will not land upon me.

Wait... fine silver suit?

So my danger magnet not only attracted the most grope-tastic person in the bar, it had actually sandwiched me between the bad touch guy and a psycho killer. Thanks, life! You rock!

Sarcasm. It's not just for the hopeless.

When psycho silver suit boy finds I've gotten away, he lets out this horribly unflattering grunt and lunges at me again. With a quick swipe of my Mercy-stick, I am able to deflect his blade. And, instead of skewering me into the dingy grey wall behind me, the blade slits a hole across my brand new, thousand dollar dress. Oh, and it took some skin with it, but seriously, I paid a grand for this costume and silverback here just ruined it! Or, does this just make it seem even more retro now, Katie?!?

FREELANCER

He swipes at me again and I bat it away with Mercy. However, I am far too preoccupied with what he's done to my slutty costume. That's all I get with this awesome dress! Awesome? Slutty? OK, it's a little of both – but it's mine! You don't get to keep a lot of nice things in my line of business, but dude, one freakin' night! Another swipe with the blade – this one too close for comfort. I can feel the cold sharp pain as it separates the flesh of my arm and tugs at another corner of my dress. Leaping back and landing flat against the alley's wall, I can feel my dress tear from the awkward maneuver.

Panting, bleeding, my clothes ruined, and still needing to pee, I've had enough of this guy. Lowering my brow and wiping a small amount of spit from my mouth, I think it's about time psycho boy gets the strangers-with-candy treatment. He comes at me one more time, using the exact same slash he'd been using with every attack. It was an "X" formation which he alternated left to right each time. Do I slash left to right or right to left? I know! I'll just keep switching back and forth. Genius! Never thought I'd figure that out, did you, moron?

Considering I know the next slash will come from the right and sweep down to the left, I time it so Mercy clashes with his wrist as the blade approaches. When the metallic rod collides with bone, I feel the give of his wrist and watch as the dagger involuntarily ejects from his hand. He screams, calling me all manner of names that would make Mom blush, and cradles his poor wounded arm. Naturally, psycho boy thinks about chasing after the knife with his one good appendage. I neutralize that thought with a swift, upright kick from my pointed toed shoes into his family jewels. His body lurches forward and his face turns such a reddish hue I wonder if he'll pass out.

Instead of falling into unconsciousness, he stands there, swaying back and forth fairly similar to the drunky before or like some tree teetering on the verge of collapse. When he doesn't, and his back and forth motion finally begins to wear on me, I decide to speed the process along.

11

JEREMY JAYNES

Taking Mercy (get it), I touch him with her very tip. The silver suited young man, turning blue from pain if I'm not mistaken, looks at it with a horribly crinkled brow before turning his agonized eyes toward me. I flash him a smile thinly veiled in mockery before clicking the button housed on the rod's end. Maybe it's overkill. Maybe it's just the right amount. Either way, Mercy sends about five hundred thousand volts through the young man. He flings from his standing position and lands like the refuse he is in the trashcans behind. Crumbling into a twitching mess, our stalker friend will be out for a while.

The echo of multiple feet hitting pavement resonates through the alley, telling me Dust and Katie's personal security are headed my way. No time to collect myself, I search the ground for Katie, figuring she has to be nearby. Thankfully, I had surprised psycho boy and he didn't have time to complete whatever sickly plan he had in store. There, tucked away like some prized doll, I find Katie lying just passed some boxes a few feet away. Unconscious, but otherwise unharmed, she looks as pretty as a picture – and she's breathing to boot. That's always a plus.

Taking a smelling salt from the tiny kit I keep strapped to my thigh, I wake her the gentlest way I'm able... running salt under her nose... then slapping her.

Then again.

What? She insulted me. I saved her life. We're even.

As the security team scoops up the woozy girl and Penny alerts emergency services, I can't help taking another look at that white knife. I could care less about silver suit boy. Dust is currently stepping on the back of his neck, while possibly over-aggressively putting him in wire handcuffs. I may have neglected to tell Dust I broke his wrist. Oops. A total accident, I swear.

Anyway, knowing I can't touch the knife, I take out my thumb phone (guess what size it is?) and snap a couple of photos. This dagger, which seems too long to be a knife but too short to be a sword, is the strangest I've ever seen. The handle and the blade seem to be made of the same glossy pearl. In fact, the more I study it, the more I believe it may be one solid piece carved from the same material. Switching to 3-D video, I use Mercy to flip the dagger over so I can see it from all sides. Moving in even closer, I note the faintest etchings on the handle and blade.

12

FREELANCER

"Glad to see you'll still get paid, Ms. Freeman," Ketchum calls as he appears at the alleyway entrance.

Dust, still holding the stalker-boy on the ground, is looking at me as if he needs permission to tear the Scot apart. I blink and grimace – my own version of asking him to hold tight. Furious at Ketchum's sudden reappearance, but doing my best to play it off, I stand from the knife and straighten my once precious garments. Strolling to him in the most seductive way I can muster with multiple slash marks, frizzy hair, and blood running down my arm, I bat my pretty little, innocent girl scout eyes at him, sashay my booty one last time... then I take a swing as hard as I can.

I know my punch is on target. I know it should connect. But instead, I find his hand pulling my arm forward while he steps away. My own momentum is turned against me, and I find myself facing the completely wrong direction, as Ketchum stands behind me. Right, he's not a G-man.

He's a Scottish ninja.

Add that to the list of possibilities.

At least I was able to confirm Ketchum has some training behind him. Crap. Dust saw everything and is darting our way. Hastily, I step between Dust and Ketchum, literally holding my friend back. He'd take the shadowy man apart right now without a second thought. But I need him calm, and I need our shadow to believe he's got the best of us – because, frankly, he does at the moment. But until we know more about him, I'd at least like to keep things cordial.

"Well," I say with a finger in Ketchum's face, and Dust edging over my shoulder, "Maybe I will get paid, but you owe me a new dress."

Kicking what little dirt at him I can from the grimy pavement, I walk away, pulling Dust along with me. My personal off-duty policeman doesn't stop eyeballing Ketchum until we're past Katie and halfway down the alley. Thank God that's over.

As we near the street, Dust wraps me in his big leather coat, and I rest my head on his shoulder. The adrenaline, which had been competing with my own red blood cells for dominance, has finally begun to wear off, and I am finally able to feel the moist cool air coming from the coast. The humid night reminds me of something else I really need.

"Dust?" I ask from his shoulder.

"Yeah, Free," he returns. "What's up?"

And, with all the lady-like charm I can gather, I ask, "Can I pee now?"

13

Chapter 2
I am Woman, Hear Me Snore

"Face down, ass up? I'm not sure what that says about you, Free," is the way my loving Penny wakes me.

I can feel a warm pool of saliva drowning my barely exposed cheek, while the goose-down throw pillow from our couch mashes against the rest of my face. Wearily, my eyes flicker open and my arms stretch across the material below me, confirming I have indeed been asleep on our fluffy stone-white couch. Shifting my weight, it somewhat registers why Penny made her comment. While my face is securely implanted in the pillow, my rear-end is sticking straight into the air. I remembered coming into the apartment last night, throwing down my keys and purse, removing my jewelry and shoes, and then collapsing head first into our couch. From the looks of things, I didn't move after that except to pull a blanket over my arse. Seems my little destroyed cocktail dress didn't provide a lot of warmth down there.

My eyes shut and words muffled by the pillow, I mumble, "Well, at least my natural instinct to stay warm kicked in." I say this in reference to my covered, upturned caboose.

"No, sweetie," Penny returns. The smell of the coffee she sips is nearly intoxicating. "That's because of Grant."

My eyes perk open as I say, "Grant's here?"

Penny's little brother – my shaggy-haired Grant – had been our tag-along since I'd known her. He was fifteen, full of hormones, and made Penny look downright social by comparison. I loved the boy dearly, but he was so accident-proned that putting the two of us together was a travesty waiting to happen. Actually, I'm probably over-stating. However, to date, he's stabbed or pricked me with two forks, three knives, scissors, and three pens – not that I'm counting. Not to mention all the times we've bumped into each other and dropped a book, can, jug, or what-have-you on me and/or the floor. And then there are the doors he's hit me with and the drawers and the... well, I think you get the point. It's not an every day thing, but it happens often enough.

"Yeah, he stayed in the spare bedroom last night so he could hit the campus library today," Penny says, sipping that caffeinated nectar of the gods from her cup. "I woke up to the loud crashes of him tripping over our dining stools. Something you slept through."

The way our apartment is laid out, our living room and kitchen are practically one room. The only thing separating them is a small island, desk, or bar – depending on how you look at the unique piece of furniture. Built by one of my first official clients, he didn't have the money to pay, so he made up for it with his fine carpentry skills. The bar is our water cooler, dining room, headquarters, and lounge all rolled into one. White with glasses hanging above, the four foot tall island houses a touch face holographic 3-D computer in the black glass top – not unlike the small glass tablets Penny carries around with her. She's linked it and all of her many computers (don't ask me why she has multiple) to the NASA inspired brain stashed away in our spare bedroom. My girl is actually so paranoid she hides it behind an alarmed fake wall in our closet.

For two girls barely a year out of high school and located in New L.A., this place is a palace. A thousand square feet, three bedrooms, one full bath, and all ours. A few more Freelancing gigs and we may even trade up.

Penny continues, "I come in here to find Grant with his deer-in-headlights look, stammering about getting a glass of water." With a cocked eyebrow she adds, "That's when I finally see your white butt practically waving *hello* to both of us. So I threw a blanket over it and sent my hormonally challenged brother back to bed."

This comment, like some resurrection spell for the dead, finally gets me to right my weary self. Rolling my overly-friendly derrière onto the couch cushion, I reluctantly pull my heavy head from the pillow. My hair, frizzy as could be, and make-up running everywhere, I feel as though I lost that fight last night, or at the least, feel like I caught the wrong end of Mercy. Glancing at the pillow housing my drool collection, I notice my makeup caked into the pristine white fabric. As nonchalant as my lethargic body will allow, I flip it over, hoping not to lose any more brownie points with my best friend this morning.

"Sorry," is all I can seem to choke out with my dry throat. My saliva reservoir had obviously emptied onto the pillow.

"Don't be," Penny says pouring another cup of that wondrous coffee. "You probably made his year. 'Course, his absolute love and devotion to you has probably just hit an all time high."

15

I hear a ceramic cup slide across the counter. I've yet to open my eyes wide enough to turn around. The sun coming through the blinds practically demands they stay closed.

"Now," Penny continues, "Drink this coffee I just poured so we can have a coherent conversation before you wash that pillow and I leave for class."

Should have known she'd see the spit and makeup stained pillow. I'm off the couch and to the counter before my eyes can adjust to the light. Scooping the warm cup into my shaking hands, I lift the brim to my nose for a smell just before sipping. The hot liquid is absolutely divine.

"You are such a drama queen," Penny jibes like only she can.

My girl, Penny, is about my size and as far as I'm concerned, prettier than I'll ever be. Then again, she says the same about me. I just think she never puts herself together as much as I do. Her idea of fashion is stealing my clothes (which I only buy for jobs) and pulling her auburn hair into a ponytail. A nerd through and through, she's all about computer science and technology and far more organized than me. She's also the only person I've ever met that truly understands me – aside from my mother. Pen knows all the right buttons to push and what combinations will do the most damage. And you'd think that would make her a bad friend. On the contrary, I couldn't ask for a better Gal Friday. She encourages me when I need it most and busts my chops when my ego might go wild if unchecked. If Freelancer, Inc. is a ship, Penny is the rudder.

"Now, down to business – First and most importantly, Worthington's money came through this morning."

See what I mean. Organized.

"Yay..." my voice quietly echoes from my coffee cup.

"Second, Dust called and said the stalker is booked and not looking at bail."

This time, I'm too busy ingesting my warm, welcoming brew to let out any real words, so I just thumbs up in approval.

"Third, it's your turn to take the trash out."

My thumb immediately turns down in reply.

"And fourth," she continues cheerfully, "Your mom is on her way over and I'm getting in the shower as soon as Grant gets out of the bathroom."

FREELANCER

Penny hurriedly exits her stool and makes her way to the toaster, as if hiding from her last comment. Her blurted fourth item came out so fast, it hasn't exactly registered in my foggy head. I sip my coffee one last time before her words reach the reasoning center of my brain.

"My who is what? Wait? Mom?"

Looking down at my bandaged arm and stomach, tossed hair, and ruined dress, I realize she cannot see me like this. Fast as I can, I dart from my stool, kicking it backwards a few inches by accident, while I make for the hallway that leads to our bedrooms and bath. Shimmying my once cute little red dress over my head, I try not to fall due to the lack of vision. Just as my shredded red confines reach their apex, ensuring I'm not only completely blind but also in nothing more than my underwear, I begin to pass the bathroom door. As I do, I hear the familiar screech of hinges and the bathroom door's humid seal broken.

I stop dead in my tracks.

"Grant?" I ask.

I can't see a thing. My dress is still firmly over my head and face, but I know he's standing there.

The boy, something obviously in his mouth impairing his speech, answers meekly, "Yeah?"

Because it's him and because it's me, I ask this next question. If it was anyone else, I might not. But I've known him so long, I'm just playing the odds.

"Sweetie," I say without budging. "What are you pointing at me right now?"

Penny let's out a loud laugh from the kitchen. Obviously, she is thinking of something more or less Freudian he might be pointing at my half-naked body.

"Um..." he slurs out in hesitation, but finally owns up in some manliness. "In my defense, it's not very sharp."

Our accident-proned Grant, who happens to be just a few inches shorter than me, has emerged from the bathroom with a pencil sticking out of his mouth. The eraser end, which he relishes chewing, is in his teeth, while the finely sharpened point is, of course, about an inch from my jugular.

I can hear Penny's slippered feet shuffle up from behind. She immediately removes the pencil from her brother's mouth, covers his eyes so he's no longer staring at her exhibitionist roommate's underwear clad body, and shuffles him off to the kitchen.

If last night didn't do it, then this certainly made his year.

"What did we say about you carrying sharp objects around, Free?" Penny chastises.

Removing the dress completely, I look back to make sure Grant is no longer enjoying the view. Penny's got him by the shoulders like some scolding mother dragging a disobedient child from the department store. Poor kid. My sympathies only last a moment though because once I see the bathroom door open, and Penny occupied, I waste no time and I dart inside.

"Hey, how was I supposed to know she was standing in front of the bathroom door... in her black underwear... half naked...?" I hear the young man defensively trailing before I close the bathroom door. There was just a dash too much excitement in his voice during that last bit.

Ew.

* * *

Five minutes later, I reemerge. Hair pulled into a ponytail (as much of it as I can anyway), makeup removed, and now wearing a bathrobe, I feel confident this will appease my mother much more than the "beat down prostitute" look I had been sporting. Making my way back to the kitchen, I see Penny flash Grant a photo from her 3-D tablet computer.

Grant, pouring juice at the refrigerator, enthuses, "That's so wicked."

"Wicked is one word for it," Penny says not as enthusiastically, turning the pad back to face her. She drags the image from the pad and enlarges it on the bar surface computer.

As I get closer, I realize she's looking over the pictures I took of that weird white dagger. Grant returns the juice carton to its rightful home in the refrigerator before joining his sister at the counter. By the time he reaches the bar, she's already moved on to viewing photos of the perp.

"I'm gone for three minutes," I joke of her going through my phone's photos, "And you guys start going through my stuff."

"What?" Penny returns in kind. "I've already read your diary. I needed some other way to pass the time."

"Dude, Free, that knife of yours looks like the Blade of Everending from Fantasy War," Grant says with boyish excitement. "It's so boddin' cool."

"Knife of..." I start to say, then realize I just stepped in nerd. "Seriously, Grant, you have to stop playing those online massively gamey video game thingies and make some real friends."

"That's not fair. I have real friends," he defends. "They're just... not from around here. They're in Canada and Germany and China and Australia and all over. They're my guild, but they *are* real people."

"What the hell is a guild?" I ask, wondering if he's making up words. "Is that like a Stone Mason or something?"

Penny, rolling her eyes, chimes in, "Oh Lord, this will lead nowhere good."

"They're my team," Grant explains as if I should know. "They're my friends I play with online."

"So why don't you just call them a team?" I ask with the same attitude. Damn, we really are like brother and sister sometimes.

"Because that's not what it's called," Grant argues. "Why don't you call Mercy *Metal Wand*? That's what it is."

Defensive, but mostly joking, I reply, "First of all, Mercy is a she. And second, she is a member of this family and a friend. And she will be treated as such."

We can hardly keep up the argumentative charade before Grant and I begin laughing at the absurdity of our conversation. Penny simply shakes her head and mutters something about "idiots" under her breath. She continues flipping through the photos from last night.

"I'm sorry," Grant says in good humor. "I'll apologize to Mercy the next time I see her. Maybe I'll take her to the movies or something to make up for it."

"Okay," I joke. "But don't get fresh. Hands on your own popcorn, mister."

Derisively, Penny adds with some blue humor, "Aren't they always?"

Ouch. And Grant, embarrassed in front of the girl he likes, retreats to the refrigerator as if refilling his juice glass will somehow be so distracting I won't remember Penny's comment.

19

"Honestly though, little brother," Penny continues with about fifty percent less sarcasm. "You should get some friends you could actually go to the movies with – without the added cost of a plane ticket."

"I see them in video chat all the time, and we watch movies online together," he defends with a full glass of juice. "And it's not like sitting in a dark theater, not talking, is socializing. I don't see the difference."

He looks to me with his baby blues as if I'll support his introverted ways. I can only crinkle my brow and shake my head, indicating he's not winning me over.

Looking to Penny with my sarcastic dark eyes, I say, "I blame his computer nerd sister for this."

Checking her watch, Penny cries, "Speaking of – crap!"

She grabs the backpack lying next to her and zips it up lickety-split. Once it's closed, she jumps from the stool and grabs my purse sitting at the edge of the counter. Rifling through my belongings, I don't even bother to ask what she's looking for. Before my sleepy mind can postulate a query, out comes Mercy.

"Got class until late," She says, zipping the stick into the front of her pack. "Gonna have to borrow Mercy for the walk to the bus stop tonight."

"You two really need to get a car," Grant advises with his many years of experience.

"Thanks," I sarcastically reply.

"And if my little brother wants to come with me to the bus stop," Penny says, pretty much demanding he come with her, "Then he needs to leave with me now... that is, unless, Free would like to show you more body parts before we go?"

I think Grant and I are turning the same shade of embarrassed red. Penny throws me a smirk, knowing there's not a single retort adequate to defend my unintentional actions of the last few hours. She heads to the front door, which is located just off to the side of the kitchen. In a grand, inviting gesture, she swings the door wide open. Taking his cue, Grant sheepishly scurries out. No eye contact with me and no "goodbye." He's far too embarrassed to mind manners. His sister's ability to concurrently humiliate both of us is a damning talent to say the least. As Penny begins to exit as well, smug smile on her face, I hear her little brother say from the hall, "Oh hey, Ms. Freeman!"

Penny's eyes meet mine, and her smile becomes so deeply satisfied I wonder if it will affect her mood all day. She lingers at the door, waiting for my mother to cross the threshold. And... here she comes.

"Hey, Jennifer!" Penny says overly-enthused. It's not as if Pen's actually unhappy to see my mother. Heck, they're practically BFF's – hence she calls Mom "Jennifer." She just really gets off on putting me through the ringer, especially on days like this when I seem to do nothing but screw up. Come to think of it, that's kind of shitty. I may have to address this with her.

Then again, I did flash her little brother... twice... so I might deserve everything I get.

As my Gal Friday exits the apartment, she passes the prettiest dame this side of New Beverly. Through the front door strolls in the most perfect hour glass figure you ever saw. She's got long, full brown hair, pouty, come-hither lips, and deep brown eyes that always hint of secrets. She's the kind of woman Sam Spade would have turned away for being too stunning, believing she'd surely double cross him, and the type most men would kill for. Even though approaching the age of forty, she doesn't look a day over thirty and hasn't for some time.

And she happens to be my mother.

I'm so proud.

Making my way to the coffee pot, attempting not to stare at how beautiful and bouncy her hair looks today, I say "Hey, Mom. Want some?"

"Morning, Lizzy," she says, entering the kitchen. After a swift kiss on the cheek, she tosses her purse right next to mine on the counter. Like mother like daughter. Mom, tall like me but with dark brown hair instead of black, is constantly mistaken for my sister. Literally, people do not believe us when we tell them she's my mother.

Twelve ounces of class in a ten ounce champagne flute, she moves with the elegance of a woman with means – though she hardly has any. She likes to say all of my grace comes from her, while the frayed edges come from Dad. She doesn't talk about him much, but I know Mom grew up in private school, while Dad was a rough and tumble sort. The idea of talking about him, though all these years later, is still too much for her. Whenever I do work up the nerve to ask, she stands me in front of the mirror and says, "Those pretty eyes are mine, cute nose too, but that sly grin of yours and dirt on your cheek – that's all your father."

21

A drop dead stunner and cool to boot, I couldn't bring a boy home without him fawning all over her. But as much as I love her – and I truly do – growing up with the "hot mom" was just not what a girl needed. I had enough boy trouble without adding my temptress mother to the mix. No, really. Serious boy trouble. Have we met? Most girls date the bad boy who goes to jail for getting into a fight or shoplifting or some stupid teenage crime.

One of mine was tried as an adult for assault with a deadly weapon.

The other is on death row.

Gotta love Mom though. She's the reason I grew up strong enough to handle these crazy situations and able to retain my sanity. I love her to death.

God, I wish she wasn't here.

She takes a look at my brewing lover in a glass pot.

"No, I'm... fine," she says, leering at my coffee cup. "I'm trying to quit caffeine."

I look at her cross-eyed. One of my many unique talents, I'll admit.

"Don't give me that," she laughs. "Someday, you'll start doing things you never dreamed too."

Half the time Mom acts like a girl my age, the other half she pretends she's some dawdling grandmother. I can't help wonder if that's because she has a danger-magnet for a daughter, causing her at times to feel aged beyond her years. Similarly, I guess I feel older than I really am, considering I'm so much more equipped to handle the world than most girls my age. Penny says Mom and I are just alike. I don't see it.

"Good God," Mom says passing the trashcan. "Did you guys dump a corpse in there? You could at least have the decency to bury it."

Okay, there might be some passing similarities.

We pull up to the counter where Penny and I had been sitting, and I readjust my bathrobe. I've flashed enough people for one day, and I don't need Mom seeing either of my bandages or one of the many bruises I surely have. As I tighten my cottony belt, I notice an appraising eye on me.

"So what's going on?" she asks as plainly as waiving a loaded gun around.

Why? Why does she have to know every time?

"Nothing," I return in a quick, innocent manner, indicating I am very much guilty of something.

"You were Freelancing last night," she says with some knowing in her voice.

What the hell? Did I get ratted out?

"Who told you?" I exclaim.

Squinting her loving, analytical eyes, she advises, "You did. Just now." She relents the sternness of her words for some humor. "Like you always do. I can't believe you still fall for it after all this time."

"Damn it, Mom," I say taking an agitated drink of my wake-up juice.

"So what was this one?" she asks. "Or, do I want to know?"

Careful to avoid the dangerous aspects, I advise, "Well, it involved a girl, a stalker, and a posh rich-kids club."

That comment earns me an upshot eyebrow. I can see she's curious to know more, but a little afraid to ask. Mom never wanted me to Freelance. Good God, I thought she was going to have a conniption when I first told her, which – like what happened here – was completely by accident. She threatened to cut me off, to never let me have another red cent!

OK, this right here tells you where I get the crazy.

1) We don't have money. Mom's a real estate agent. It's how we moved so much, and it put food on our table, but money? No.

2) She saw all the crazy things I went through as a kid (though she argues I still am a kid – different conversation for a different day), but still claims I'm normal.

3) Even after number 2 (above), she's the most open minded person I know... but somehow she still doesn't claim to see the danger attracted to me! I'm dead serious when I say she was willing to believe Grant when he thought he saw a UFO, but thought it was all in my head when I claimed it was my danger magnet which caused us to pick the one subway train that derailed.

"Well," she begins with the sarcasm I get from her, "At least that might explain the hair."

23

I primp my extremely messy, jagged locks pondering just how bad it might really look. I kind of liked my hair. Dropping her humor, Mom is very obviously considering asking another question. Before she does, she casually stands from the counter and walks to our cabinets where she begins rifling around.

Pulling out a coffee mug, she says with a crinkled nose, "Maybe I will have some."

Now I know she's upset.

As she pours herself a black cup (not even sugar, Mom?), she asks calmly, "So who was the client?"

"Girl's name was Katie Worthington. Her dad's…" I forget what he does, "…he's like the Archduke of Money or something."

"So you kept her safe?" she says, still holding the coffee pot though her mug is full.

"Yeah, guy's in jail," I reply without ego. "Her dad's grateful though. His payment will pay off the apartment for the rest of the year."

Mom replaces the pot and ambles back to the counter. She cautiously reseats herself, attempting to not spill her full to the brim cup. Holding the mug as though it's warming her fingers, she sips the coffee.

Switching gears completely, out of the blue she asks, "You're still taking classes, right?"

"Yes," I reply with a dash of daughterly attitude. "I'm even doing pretty well."

After the first semester of college, I realized I was not built to sit in a classroom. That's when I decided to start Freelancing part-time and take courses online. I call it being responsible. Mom calls it… well, not as responsible. But, hey, she never even went to college. She had me instead. So how she can even…

"So this job last night," she says, switching back again. Mom tends to do this during our Freelancing conversations. She likes to put off certain questions by asking others. "Did you at least carry a gun?"

I sip my coffee and don't say a word. While Mom may like to put off asking questions, my preference is to put off answering them.

"Oh, Lizzy, tell me you got your permit?" She asks, somewhat startled. "You told me you were getting one!"

My mother might be the only parent I know who actively campaigns for her daughter to carry a firearm. Gotta love her.

"I am," I honestly reply. "I just haven't sent the paperwork in yet."

"Elizabeth Freeman!" she chastises. I know I'm in trouble when she uses the full name. "It's bad enough you have this superhero fantasy in your head, but to go out without any sort of protection—."

"I brought Mercy!" I interject. "And Dust!"

The look on her face tells me she is not impressed by my honesty. I suddenly feel as though I'm eight years old again and I have just been through my second house fire. We thought that one was my fault for about six months, until the report came back about the faulty wiring. Sidebar: Oddly, none of the houses we lived in ever burned down, only my friends' homes ever caught fire... or met some other gruesome ends. However, I'm a semi-grown woman now, and I need to accept my choices – not some eight year-old girl who needs to be told she's done nothing wrong.

Defensive, I say, "Hey, I've earned a good reputation!"

Moderately true.

"I'm always careful!"

A modest fib.

"And I never take chances!"

An out and out lie.

Mom's eyes burrow into me, while mine, having just been bold enough to defend my lifestyle, retreat like a scared kitten to the cup of coffee in front of me. My guilt is very transparent.

As sheepish as poor Grant earlier, I advise, "I'll mail out the paperwork today."

Chapter 3
Through Rain or Snow

As I stand in line at the Post Office, I begin to wonder if I chose the right ensemble for the day. My shirt, black with evil red eyes where my boobs are and the back designed to look ripped open, exposing my skin (wore an invisible bra today to not appear too slutty), was meant for my Katie-guarding persona. If stalker-boy hadn't made his move last night, this morning I'd have gone for coffee with Katie, wearing something like this. I've also got several other pieces of clothes, about a week's worth, in case her situation took longer than one night. To date, a Freelancing gig has yet to last much longer than a few days. When you've got me around, the problem seems to find you sooner rather than later.

The shirt, while kind of cool, is nothing compared to my pants. A few weeks back I was playing myself off as this edgy wanna-be rockstar type. And whenever I take on a new persona, I typically study current trends and the famous people wearing them. In this case, I picked this fairly popular electric metal singer (think Madonna meets Ozzy Osborne) who has made a few waves with her fashion choices. Thing is, this girl has a great figure and she likes to show it off. I chose her because – for the type anyway – she doesn't go overboard. I tend to call it "rock sexy" or "conservative slut." So what does this mean about the pants I'm wearing? It means they have no sides.

In case you're as lost on this concept as I was, I'll repeat.

They have no sides. From the edge of my behind to the bottom of my pants the sides spider-web into thin lines of white and blue fabric, as if the jeans have been pulled apart. The lines are thick in most places so your skin isn't completely exposed, but in other places it separates. In a way, the design is extremely inventive because it presents an air of sexiness or even nudity, but really the jeans show much less than even a skirt. Of course, they are skin tight, adding to their provocative nature.

26

FREELANCER

When I'm on the job, the sultry, offensive, heck – sometimes smelly clothes are all a part of the persona – they don't represent me. So, on my day off, why wouldn't I wear jeans so tight they feel like a second skin? It's not like when I'm not working – when I'm unable to hide behind a persona – I'm self-conscious or anything. Oh, wait... I am extremely self-conscious. Right, almost forgot.

What kills me is, every time I take a step, I want to glance back to make sure my pants haven't ripped open. They're jeans made of strung out threads! Then again, as I contemplate this, I realize all jeans are just a series of strung together threads. Hmm, maybe I'm not giving the designer enough credit. Tight as they are, they are pretty comfortable. Really, they fit me perfectly and I can barely tell I'm wearing them... except for the constant paranoia of feeling inappropriately dressed for some reason. Thing is, my dress last night showed a hundred times more leg.

Oy, damn you self-conscious girl-mind! I just need stamps. Why did I get dressed at all? That's it. I'm stealing my clothes from Penny from now on. She likes to steal my stuff anyway.

The line moves. Thank God. Taking a step forward, I get that uneasy chill of someone's eyes falling upon me – an unrelenting and unwanted stare. Too many times have I felt this look, and too many times have I seen how this ends. I don't think I can take this today.

Oh, please don't be another stranger-with-candy. Please don't be another stranger-with-candy. Please don't be another – I glance behind.

And, without a doubt, I have my winner. Tall, thinning blond dude in his late thirties and wearing some weird logo t-shirt, his arm is draped as if it has nothing better to do except hang at his side. Looking closer though, I can see the thumb phone cradled in his palm. The device, aiming low and in my direction, makes the quiet, distinct click of a photo being snapped. This cannot be good. Casually, I look down to the back of my pants. And, of course, the spider-webbing has shifted just enough you can see a small amount of skin at the highest point near my canned ham.

Seriously, dude? That's all it takes for you?

I try to put the perv out of my mind, focusing on the crowd around me. When the line takes another plodding step forward, I note an older man arguing with the lady at the counter about postage. He needs something cheaper.

Don't we all.

27

There's a pretty, dark haired girl in front of me, about my age, but a bit shorter – more like Katie Worthington's height – holding a package slip, as if the postal carrier left it at her door. Like a rap across my skull, I wince as another shutter click comes from behind. My tongue's patience is wearing thin, and I bite my lip hoping it does not escape. Adjusting my jeans slightly, I hope this change will curb the man's nature, and I don't have to cause a scene. As I pull on my jeans' belt loop, I unintentionally let out an angry, huffy breath. The pretty girl in front of me, glances back, trying to understand my agitation and probably curious if it has something to do with her. As we lock eyes for a split second, I feel embarrassed that I've drawn attention to myself and give her an apologetic grimace. After all, the huff wasn't at her. However, as if the girl can see the sexual harassment written all over my mug, her eyes dart to the pervert three people back. The wave of disgust crossing her face tells me she wholly understands my plight.

"Ugh," the girl says to me very loudly and with much intent, "I guess you can't go anywhere without a pervert trying to snap pictures of you."

This girl, whatever her name might be, is my new hero.

The photo-happy man, blood draining from his face, slips the phone into his pocket and turns his guilty eyes out the window. The perv, doing such a poor job hiding his guilt, might as well whistle nonchalantly like a cartoon character. The girl's outburst has gotten everyone looking around, and most eyes are falling on him. He clears his throat and shuffles his arms.

I must be beaming because the girl looks at me with the warmest smile, touches my shoulder and says, "I'd want someone to do the same for me."

That's New L.A. for you. The amount of crime is the same as any big city, but the amount of standup people has to be three times what you'd find anywhere else. You see, we wear being a citizen of New L.A. like a badge. And the proudest people in the city are the Second Generation Angelinos. These are the people who lived in L.A. before the quake and New L.A. after. We're the survivors – the people who lifted our city out of the sea and demanded it stay afloat. Dust is 2nd Gen. Penny is too. And this girl in front of me, I have little doubt is also. Of all of us, only Dust is old enough to remember it happen, except Mom. She's full blooded Second Generation. I can only imagine how it must have been to be my age and live through it.

With natural disasters on the rise, almost every city has adopted new, sturdier building codes. None of them are perfectly hurricane/earthquake/tornado/volcano-proof, but they give it their all. About fifty percent of New L.A. is built to withstand anything, and one hundred percent of the Second Gen is built sturdier.

"Next!" the postal worker calls from the counter.

The girl, whom I still don't know her name, takes her delivery slip to the front, happy to almost be done with this agonizingly slow line. I stand there, basking in the girl's victory, feeling much better about myself than I had all day. The postal worker leaves the counter to retrieve whatever package the girl is picking up. As I watch the woman leave, I realize I can't let this girl go without thanking her and make the decision to say something before she departs. After all, this is the type of girl I need to know.

The man with the outgoing package is still haggling over the price of postage, not only causing my time at the post office to move at a snail's pace, but somewhat ensuring I'll end up using the same window as my new heroine. When the postal worker returns with the girl's package, I realize I somehow have to awkwardly thank her before she leaves. As the girl shows her ID and signs for the delivery, I try to figure out my best plan of attack. Do I step in her way like a crazy person? Tap her shoulder? Call to her?

Crap! She's leaving. The postal woman hands the girl the package, which is not much bigger than a postal box so I'm surprised it wasn't left at her door. Maybe she had to sign for it? Anyway, she's turning to walk away. What do I do?

I reach out to tap her arm, but she whisks away just out of reach, none the wiser that I wanted to thank her. However, some luck. She takes her package just down the counter, to one of the closed windows, to open her delivery. The pretty brunette is searching for a means to unwrap the box. She pulls out a set of keys and uses them as a dull knife to cut the package open. This should leave me just enough time to do my business and thank her before we both exit. Heck, if I time it right, we might walk out together.

Stepping to the window the girl had just vacated, I look to the postal clerk and say, "I would like one book of stam—."

A blood curdling shriek pierces the stuffy post office decorum, causing everyone in the room to lose a few minutes off their lifetimes. My heroine, her package open and resting on the counter, jumps back and continues to bellow a siren's high pitched wail. Forgetting my business entirely, I dart to the poor girl and take her into my arms in an effort to calm her. Her body is involuntarily shaking while tears cascade down her face. I cradle her shoulders but have no noticeable calming effect.

"Don't look in the box!" she cries. "Don't look in the box!"

Right. Poor thing is so scared, she doesn't realize she's pretty much telling me the opposite.

Another woman comes up and begins to console the girl. As she does, I slowly slip from the girl's grasp and inch to the box. At this point, I'm sure the postal cop is on his way, but I'm here and this is what I do. Peeking inside the open flaps of the plain brown package, I see the typical foamy white packing, insulating whatever lay inside. I inch closer, curiously yet cautiously, until I'm hovering above the open top. There, embedded in angelic white foam, is a vial of red liquid. Looking more closely, I can see tucked just beneath the menacing fluid, as if cradled by the magical white packing peanuts, is a photo of the girl fast asleep in her own bed. A red, dripping circle has been drawn around her.

If I'm not mistaken – and let's be frank, I'm not – the red liquid and circle around the sleeping beauty's face is blood.

I know this because it's exactly like the package Katie Worthington received.

* * *

FREELANCER

I remember the feelings that filled me every time I entered my school - the comfort of familiarity conflicting with authoritative rule in an overwhelming sea of information. This is how I feel every time I enter the New LAPD Station. I've been here often through the years, partially due to tagging along with Dust when I was a kid, and partially due to my troublesome adventures. This building is much different from the pictures I saw of the original. After the L.A. Quake, most buildings had to be torn down and rebuilt to higher standards. This station was no different. But when they rebuilt it, they made it look like something out of the 1930s – complete with round street lights out front and dark crown molding lining every room and doorway.

Acting as a central hub for all police in the city, you'd think it would be bigger. But after the quake, the city began relying on precincts to bear the burden. Police Headquarters is no different. The station is basically its own precinct, but what makes it so special is that Dust and his fellow detectives get assigned to other precincts all the time to investigate cases. They consider it an honor. I consider it a necessity.

As I enter through the old wooden and glass door, my boots clacking on the hardwood floors, the desk sergeant calls me by name. He's busy speaking to someone else but excuses himself just long enough to point me toward Dust's area. The station is filled with guys like this, welcoming faces that know me better than I know them. If you wanted to find Second Gen Angelinos, look no further than the police.

As I head down the hall, my new red leather jacket flaps against my mid-thigh, telling me the garment is serving its intended purpose nicely. The same red as the eyes on my shirt and as the cocktail dress which met its end the night before, I purchased it after leaving the Post Office. While my jeans have grown on me in the time we've spent together, going so far as to find a whole new case together, I still can't rationalize walking into the station wearing just them. Designed to look somewhat like a detective's trench coat and a bright, yet not too overpowering red, it feels in character for the girl I was last night, and the person I seem to be today.

31

JEREMY JAYNES

I enter Dust's area to find a fleet of badged gumshoes traversing the murky seas of crime armed with florescent bulbs above and bad shoes below to navigate the way. A few give me nods and smiles, while others are too busy with phone calls and paperwork to take notice. Looking to my friend's desk, I find it currently unoccupied. As I inch closer to his workspace, I catch the eye of Cliff Anderson, Dust's rookie partner. With his blazing red hair and freckles, Cliff doesn't look old enough to shave, let alone old enough to carry a gun. His hair, always horribly cut, and his suit, always too big or too small – you'd think a guy like this wouldn't make it in this station.

Flashing me a great big, goofy grin, Cliff says, "He got pulled into an interrogation room down the hall. He should be back any minute."

Down the hall, hmm? Now, I don't typically stick my nose in Dust's business. However, watching him interrogate someone, well, let's just say I like to take notes. He plays both good cop and bad cop all in one sitting. Frankly, I consider it an art. At first, he'll have the perp so terrified they think he's the man who sharpens Satan's pitch fork. Then, before it's all over, he's their father confessor taking in their every word with a shoulder to cry on. I need to learn that skill if I'm ever going to make it in Freelancing.

Making my way to the water cooler, which just so happens to be right next to the short hall leading to the interrogation rooms, I casually fill a paper cup. As I take a long, exaggerated sip of water, my eyes scan the detectives in the room. When none seem to notice the casual girl taking her casual drink, I slowly back into the doorway just before skedaddling down the hall.

The road leading to interrogation is intentionally unnerving. One of the florescent bulbs is out, another flickering, making the hall an eerie, unwanting place. Rows of wooden doors line the left and right, with nary a window and only chipped numbers marking the rooms. Now, at first I'm a bit worried I won't be able to find the room Dust is using, but that hesitation is soon quelled when I hear his angry voice echo from an open door. This rings odd if for no other reason because no cop, including Dust, would interrogate someone with a door wide open. In fact, each interrogation room has three doors – one leading from the hall, one leading into the interrogation area, and one (typically on the right or left) leading to a viewing room, sitting behind a two-way mirror. Trust me when I say I've had the privilege of being on both sides of the glass.

Still too far away to understand the conversation, I can already tell by Dust's tone this is anything but typical. This may not be an interrogation I'm walking up on, but a private conversation held away from prying ears. My internal alarm tells me I should head back to Dust's desk and wait for him there, but my curiosity is pleading I stay. Thankfully, I prove myself a better person and slowly begin creeping back down the hall, eying the door to ensure Dust doesn't suddenly burst out and find me eavesdropping. I'm just about out of earshot when I hear a loud, booming voice that stops me dead in my tracks.

"Keep this up," Ketchum says, "And you will find yourself in more trouble than you are equipped for."

"Is that a threat?" Dust returns, overpowering Ketchum's tone.

Holy crap! My feet, suddenly possessed by the spirit of unbridled perplexity, do an about face and begin inching toward Dust's room once again. Ketchum in the precinct? Visiting Dust? Arguing? My mind is awash in a sea of confusion.

"No, my good detective," Ketchum returns in his cool, Scottish accent, "It's a warning. You know more than anyone our Ms. Freeman is special."

"You've got that right," Dust defends. "And I won't see you put her in harm's way again!"

"Harm's way?" Ketchum retorts. "You bloody well know Ms. Freeman's past as well as I. She needs no help from either of us in that regard. But that's the problem right there, isn't it? You, like her mother, refuse to see what is so plainly in front of you."

Okay, at this point, I don't know whether I should bust in and ask what the hell they're talking about, or just be thankful I haven't been caught eavesdropping yet. Speaking of, the clacking of high heeled shoes are approaching from the visitor's area just down the hall.

Most cops I know don't wear heels to work (only Freelancers posing as club girls), so I'm not too terribly alarmed. Drooping my head and draping my hair over my face to obscure it, I take out my thumb phone and pretend I'm in an important texting conversation. I extend the holographic keyboard and begin typing a message addressed to no one:

PLEASE KEEP WALKING. DO NOT STOP. THAT'S RIGHT. KEEP GOING.

JEREMY JAYNES

In order to conceal my identity, I keep my head down but can't help admiring her shoes as the woman saunters by. Those are thousand dollar Marcus Nelly's she's wearing. This proves two things, she's definitely not a cop and she has my taste. I don't consider myself too terribly girly, but damn those shoes are lit. One of these days, I'm hoping I'll find a Freelancing gig that gives me an excuse to buy some.

"Don't give me that crap," Dust admonishes. "Free is just a girl with a good heart who tends to gravitate toward bad situations."

His voice tosses me right back into my dubious spying.

"Playing thickheaded doesn't suit you," Ketchum's wispy voice continues. "And I know you don't fully believe that. You've investigated her past. You know what happened to her father, don't you?"

I can't see him, but I can hear the small hesitation when Dust replies, "Her dad died the day she was born... but coincidences like that happen all the time."

"Yes," Ketchum returns. "Coincidences do. Now, tell me, how exactly did he die again? And remember, I can have you fired. Oh, and just so we're on point – that was a threat."

Wow, I'm half expecting them to rip their shirts off, oil up, and start fighting over me. Not that I'd like that sort of thing. I'm a modern woman who can take care of herself after all. I don't need hot, sweaty, half-naked, good-looking men who are each authoritative, well-muscled, and divine in their own unique ways to fight over me. Nope. Not. At. All.

"He died in the New L.A. earthquake," Dust admits in angry reluctance.

"Ah," Ketchum says, now also playing dumb. "So, on the day she was born, not only was her father killed, but the city of Los Angeles met its greatest disaster? No, no. I finally see your point, Detective. Our Ms. Freeman isn't special at all."

Uh, hitting stop on the fantasy oil-wrestling sequence, I have to fact check what I just heard. What the hell is Ketchum insinuating about me? I mean, I've been teased in the past about my birthday being the same day as the quake, but this is different. His words are hitting a little too close to home for me and I find my eyes swimming in tears I didn't know were forming. I want to storm the room, accuse Ketchum of.... well, I don't know... just being an ass, I guess... but I find my legs disobeying and unrelenting their petrified stance.

"It's all a coincidence," Dust says in a deflated tone, atypical of his brave self.

34

FREELANCER

Ketchum, with more empathy than he'd shown before, replies, "I understand why you want to believe that. Believe me, I do..."

Realizing their conversation is winding down, my atrophied feet return to life and I slowly inch my way back down the hall, listening for anything more while I'm still in earshot.

The last I hear is Ketchum say, "I'm not here because I want to be your enemy. I'm here as your friend, Detective. You need to be careful. Ms. Freeman's life is not yours."

As I reemerge in the detective's area, I'm barely cognizant of any that might have noticed my trespass. I'm too busy keeping my head down, once again using my hair for cover in order to hide the tears escaping my eyes. That bastard Ketchum. How could he say I killed my father? Or all those people? I was being born. I find trouble. I don't create it.

As inconspicuous as I can, I slip into the chair next to Dust's ugly wooden desk, removing a tissue from its top as I do. Dabbing my wet eyes, I'm thankful I decided to wear my good makeup today. Otherwise, I'd look like the Bride of Frankenstein when my friend finally arrives.

About two minutes pass, just long enough for my eyes to lose their puffy giveaway, before Dust emerges from the hall. His face is flushed and his sleeves rolled up. He's mad as could be and I love him for it. I'm truly lucky to have people like him in my life.

At first he doesn't notice my cocksure smile signaling from his desk, and he instead glares out the station windows trying to quell his internal turmoil. After a moment though, he turns toward his desk and finds my familiar mug hiding behind a mess of hair. As if a traffic signal changing from red to green, his mood shifts and a small glint of happiness flashes from his eye. He strolls to the desk, a smirk forming on his lips.

"So how much did that coat cost you?" he asks as he takes a seat. Dust loves to antagonize me about my thrifty nature to no end.

"Dude!" I return ever so eloquently. "You already got paid for last night, so you don't need to worry about it." Leave it to Dust. I cure his sour mood and he cures mine in the same instant.

"Let's... let's keep that down a bit," he says quietly. "The Captain... the precinct in general... might look the other way when it comes to me helping you, but we don't need to advertise it."

"Hey, they love having people like me around," I joke.

35

"No," Dust returns. "They love having *you* around. There are no other people like you. You made Freelancing up and got lucky when the term stuck."

Probably didn't mention that earlier. As far as I know, I'm the only Freelancer in the world, since I kind of invented it. Penny already trademarked Freelancer, Inc. We're legit!

"Cops only put up with you because of that thing with the bus."

"You mean," I begin a in a fairly loud, prideful voice, "When I saved those schoolchildren?"

Dust with an eye roll replies, "Yes, when you saved the schoolchildren."

"The schoolchildren on the flaming school bus you mean?" I reply in an increasingly enthusiastic manner.

More embarrassed than amused, Dust replies, "Yes, the schoolchildren on the flaming school bus."

Then, with all the pomp and circumstance of a cheerleading routine, I add, "You mean the schoolchildren on the flaming school bus which was rolling down a hill and I got a medal from the city for?"

This time Dust doesn't reply. He's actually biting his lip like he wants to take me over his knee and give me a proper spanking.

...That was not supposed to be sexual...

"Are you done?" he asks.

"Pretty much, yeah," I answer somewhat cheerily. "So, anyway, the reason I stopped by was I'm on another case."

"I already heard," he says flipping over a file and perusing the pages. He seems to have already lost interest in me. "And it's not the same guy."

"How did you already...?"

"Anytime your name comes up in the system, it's in your file to contact me," Dust advises while still looking over his paperwork.

"Really?" I say, unsure what to make of that.

"Yup, spoke to the lead detective that interviewed you," he continues, now all but ignoring me. "According to him, you already pointed him to a suspect. Some guy, mid thirties, balding blond hair with a thumb phone full of your skinny behind – sound familiar?"

"Oh, yeah, him..." I reply suspiciously. "Well, I changed my mind. I don't think he did it."

Hey, he could have been the perp and he could have been taking pictures of both Beth and I. Oh, and how awesome is it the cool girl in line's name is Elizabeth too?!? We completely bonded after the police arrived... and I handed her a business card... while she was in shock... and crying...

Okay, so maybe not "completely bonded" but we're getting very close.

"I kind of figured that might be the case," Dust continues, placing a piece of paper in front of me. The sheet contains a print out of gobbledygook as far as I can tell. "The blood the girl received at the Post Office doesn't match your perp from today or our collar from last night."

"Damn it," I say with real disappointment. While I wouldn't wish the psycho from last night on anyone, I really wanted him to be our guy. "He's still got to be involved."

"Without a doubt, kid," Dust says like the grown up he is. Leaning back in his chair, he finally puts his full attention back on me. "I've already interviewed our stalker, Stephen Hill, and he's not talking. All I could get out of him was, and I quote, *'You don't understand. She needs to be set free.'* It's like he's reading from the Crazy 101 manual."

"And he's got a friend," I reply morbidly.

"Yup," Dust advises. "Turns out Katie Worthington, your client, knows Stephen. So, it's more than likely your new friend knows her stalker as well. Luckily, since the cases are related, Captain's going to put me on lead with Cliff as my second."

My guard is feeling a little low when I ask, "So, what should I do?"

"Maybe talk to the girl some more," he tells me. "I'll keep looking into this weird-ass white knife our guy used and working on Stephen."

I'm not feeling especially good about this case for some reason, and Dust is picking up on it.

"Hey, we could get lucky, and the new stalker's blood could match someone in the system." Putting a conciliatory hand on my knee, he tells me, "Go see the girl, then go home until I call you. Believe it or not, you are doing everything you can."

I linger in my deflated state until I feel the urge to walk again. Uneasy with my new assignment, I reluctantly leave the squeaky old chair. Dust has already returned to his paperwork and is once again paying me little mind. Just as I'm about to make my exit from his desk, he drops the papers as if remembering something.

"Oh hey, I almost forgot, your mom called," he says. Not a surprising thing to hear considering Mom knows Dust as well as any of my friends.

"Really?" I ask preparing a witty comment. "Did you ask her out yet?"

As surprised as being shot in the foot, he replies, "Asked her what?"

"Hey, she's a good looking lady," I say with some sass. "Plus, you guys are both adults and about the same age -." I get cut off, as if I've offended him.

"Same age?" he replies with hurt feelings. "Free, I'm closer to your age than I am your mom's. I'm not even thirty yet!"

"Hmm..." I say in retrospect. "I guess Mom and I have you sandwiched right between us."

That wailing sound in the back of my mind – the one that goes off after it's too late – that would be my accidental double entendre alarm. My lips purse together and I hold my breath trying not to let another syllable escape. Dust, who caught the uncouth meaning right away, smiles wryly at my embarrassment and turns back to his paperwork.

"I won't mention to anyone," he begins, "Especially your mother, that you said that."

Unlocking my lips, I say in relief, "You are a gentleman among men."

"However," he continues with some authority, "Your mother did want me to pass something along."

Curious, I ask, "Oh, yeah?"

"Yeah," he replies. "She wanted me to ask you if you mailed the permit out okay."

Ah, damn it. I knew I forgot something.

Chapter 4
Shaken and Stirred

"Hey, are you busy?" I ask Penny on my phone's tiny earring earpiece.

"I've got another class in fifteen minutes," she answers. "So you have me for that long."

The University of Southern California's box-like trolley shuffles off its students like unwanted weight. I merge into the penguin line and follow them to the pavement outside before answering Penny. Funny enough, she's only a block or two away from me at the moment, but I know she won't have time to see me in person and a call is my only option. She's got class and I need to find Beth's dormitory.

"A couple minutes are all I need," I finally answer.

Surveying the two white stone and red brick buildings before me, I bite my lip while I try to determine which is Beth's. Weighing the evidence against each building, the street lights flick on, telling me I've already lost my day to this new case.

"Um, I need you to look up Katie Worthington, our original client, and our original stalker, Stephen Hill," I tell Pen. "Dust says they knew each other, and I'm trying to figure out how."

"That shouldn't be a problem," Penny says hesitantly. "I don't even need my tablet. I can do that on my phone. But what do you mean original? Is there a new client, or more importantly, new stalker I need to be aware of?"

"Right..." I return, having forgotten to keep her in the loop. "Good news! I have a new case!"

The phone goes quiet a moment or two before Penny finally replies, "We can't even go a day, Free. You're killing me. You are absolutely killing me. Did this person at least hire you? And by *hire* I mean they offered you money for services rendered."

Why do people insist on asking me questions I don't want to answer?

"Hey, look at that, I found our new client's dorm!" I say hurriedly.

39

Actually, I have no idea if it's the right dormitory. I'm just picking the one on the right and hoping for the best.

"Call me after class when you've looked that stuff up," I continue without letting Penny get another word out. "Love you bunches! Bye!"

Normally, I don't say "Love you bunches," but, hey, I was in a pinch.

Thankfully, my uneducated guess pays off and I soon find myself wandering down Beth's hall. Typical of a female dorm in the summertime, life is sparse and territorial, causing the few girls around to be leery of a new presence roaming their halls. And with it being a co-ed dorm, that goes double for the girl-crazed guys which leer at every female passerby. Having only been a full-time student for a semester, I'm reminded why I don't miss the dorms. There is little privacy and too many girls making snippy comments about wardrobe and hair for my liking. I round another corner in the baby blue hallway, one of the many neutral colors I've come across in the building thus far, and see at the far end room 407 – Beth's room. I approach the door to knock, adjusting my clothes and hair a little before I do.

What? I'm nervous. I don't have a lot of friends and Beth is cool.

As if avoiding my fist, which was about to pummel it with my not-so-mighty knock, the door pulls away from my knuckles. My hand is frozen in its knocking state, and my eyes are wide and full of awkward surprise. A woman, not noticing my presence at first, is attempting to exit the room when she turns to find me standing there. The red-headed woman, in a conservative, yet shapely red business suit, roughly 40 years old, and a bit of a dame, looks just as surprised to see me as I am her. She jumps, startled by my presence. As if mimicking the woman, I follow suit, jumping a moment after her.

Real professional of me.

"I'm sorry," the woman apologizes. "I didn't realize -."

I cut her off saying, "No, no, my fault. I was coming by to see Beth."

Each of us is stammering over the other, completely apologizing for scaring the begeezus out of one other. Really, I'm not sure anyone is to blame.

"Free?" A tiny, scared voice questions from within the room.

FREELANCER

The startled lady in red moves from the doorway, allowing me passage. Inside I find Beth sitting cross-legged in her tiny dorm room, drooping on the lower half of a bunk bed. She clutches a stuffed dog in one hand and a tissue in the other. My heart goes out to her. Inching further into the room, I move to the girl's side. In a surprise to me (less so than the door opening, mind you), she reaches out and wraps her arms around my neck. I take a place on the bed and return the show of affection. The woman, whom I can only assume is Beth's mother at this point though they look nothing alike, places her hand over her heart as if touched by the moment.

"Good," the woman says. "I was afraid to leave Beth alone. I'm glad you came."

Beth, relinquishing her grip, introduces, "Ms. Sullivan, this is Free. She's a…" Beth is searching for the term *Freelancer* but cannot find it. Considering what she's been through today, I can let it slide.

"I'm a friend," I finish for her.

Even if I did explain what I do for a living, there are a lot of people out there who either don't get it or think I'm joking. After all, how can a girl my age be this successful? To which, I can reply, "My lease is paid for a year. How's yours?"

The woman seems truly relieved to see me. Even if I am a sucker for a wounded soul, making me a… well… *sucker* sometimes, my bullshit detector typically works just fine on the non-teary-eyed folk. I can tell the lady in red did not want to leave our girl.

"Ms. Sullivan was faculty at my old school," Beth informs me. "Now, she's just a good friend."

"A friend you can always call when you need me," she says with earnest. "Free, do you happen to live around here?"

I'm not sure where this is going and Beth seems put off, but I'll bite.

"Not far at all, actually," I reply. "Just off campus."

"Ms. Sullivan…" Beth says in a huffy breath.

"You are not staying here alone," she demands. "Someone needs to be with you."

"Hold on, Beth, where are your parents?" I ask in utter disbelief they wouldn't be around.

41

I don't realize until it's too late that I'm striking a nerve. Beth's despairing eyes find another wrung in hell, sent there by a girl with the best of intentions. I'm mortified as she begins obviously fighting off more tears. Her grip on her fluffy companion tightens as do her lips. My only life preserver is standing in the doorway wearing thousand dollar Marcus Nelly shoes.

Seriously, am I the only person who doesn't have those boddin' shoes?

"Free," Ms. Sullivan carefully begins. Beth's wounded eyes turn to her, as if she too is awaiting an explanation for her parents' absence. "Let's speak in the hall a moment."

If this woman wasn't a teacher, I'd feel rude leaving Beth. But somehow, her teacher's authority seems to extend into our adult lives. As soon as she asked to see me in the hall, I felt like I had to go or else face detention. We excuse ourselves from the room and exit. Ms. Sullivan carefully closes the door behind us, as if it slammed, it might shatter the girl inside.

"Beth's parents…" Ms. Sullivan attentively explains as we step away from the closed door. "Are not in the picture at the moment. She doesn't have the best of relationships with her father. I alerted him hours ago but have yet to see him arrive or even so much as call."

"Oh," I reply. "I didn't know."

Ms. Sullivan with a conciliatory hand on my shoulder advises, "You wouldn't. Beth doesn't talk about it much. However, while she's one of the strongest girl's I've had the privilege of working with, she also needs someone to help her right now."

"I can do that," my heart says, pushing my brain aside.

Ms. Sullivan studies my eyes a moment. She gazes into them as if looking for some flicker of doubt in my resolve. Finding no weaknesses in my armor, she places both hands on my shoulders in a motherly gesture of encouragement.

"Good," she says. "I'll leave you my card in case you need me."

* * *

FREELANCER

Ms. Sullivan has been gone for ten minutes when Beth decides to freshen up in the restroom. Once she returns, we'll head to my place for the night. I can't help feeling awful for this girl. Unlike Katie, who seemed to blow off the whole affair, Beth is appropriately terrified. The last stalker never had a chance to carry out his plan, but it's obvious he would have.

Looking over the numerous pictures of Beth's high school friends on the walls, most of which I learned are either vacationing or are in the middle of moving to their new colleges, I feel sorry for the girl. Stuffed in the corner of those smiling faces is her single family photo. Her father is standing far off to the left with a chiseled chin and tweed jacket. He dominates the photo as he stretches his arm around his wife, leaving Beth untouched in the corner. She stands there with a glorious smile, surrounded by family yet alone. I can't help wonder what would cause such a rift between her and her father. No matter how serious the argument, a situation like this should warrant a parental response.

Her senior yearbook, begging to be picked up, has been blatantly tossed atop a stack of notes and schoolbooks – mathematics, theology, network design all littering her desk. Not one to deny a request, I lift the yearbook from its scholarly perch and open the cover. On the white bounded first pages, where all her friends scribbled differing comments before the end of their school term, I find myself making assumptions about the people and relationships shared.

LOVE YOU! KEEP IN TOUCH!
xxoo Alison xxoo
They probably never spoke again.

WHATEVER YOU DO, DON'T FORGET YOUR BLOOMERS!
-Linda-
I'll assume it's an inside joke…. about underpants.

I'LL SEE YOU NEXT YEAR, PROMISE!
-Katie-
A total lie.

JEREMY JAYNES

THANK YOU FOR EVERYTHING! YOU HAVE NO IDEA HOW
WONDERFUL A DANCER YOU ARE. I WILL ALWAYS BE HERE IF
YOU NEED ME!
-Eric-

Ah, the crush that got away... that will come out of the closet by
Thanksgiving break.

As I continue to peruse the pages of her classmates' life-scarring
photographs, I start to wonder about where my graduating class ended
up. Actually, come to think of it, I really don't care. I prefer to worry
about my more immediate friends. In fact, I probably need to check on
Beth. She's been gone almost fifteen minutes.

Curiously, I exit the room and make my way down the hall toward
where I believe the bathrooms are located. On my way, I pass a girl and
ask if she's seen Beth head this way. I'm not especially shocked when
the girl says "no." I don't take inventory every time Penny walks through
the apartment and our hall is a quarter this long.

Upon reaching the white tiled bathroom, surprisingly clean for so
many girls to use, I don't see Beth at first glance. I figured she'd be
standing at one of the six sinks lined by the doorway, wiping her puffy
eyes and face. With Beth not at the sinks, my next thought is she might
have locked herself in one of the stalls, looking for a few moments'
solitude. Moving further into the restroom, I begin, begrudgingly,
checking for feet under the stall doors. Being a girl, this is a common
practice when the doors seem to close on their own, and you don't want
to be the person barging in on someone. As I lean over, my hair nearly
scraping the thankfully clean floor, I keep expecting to hear a whimper
from one of the closed doors. The only problem with this scenario, I've
reached the last stall, and there's no one in here.

I dart from the bathroom, nearly knocking over a girl on my way out. Barely breaking stride, I ask the stumbling girl if she's seen Beth. The young coed has no idea who I'm talking about and is probably wondering if I'm on drugs. Passing door after door, my hurried feet make muted thuds on the carpeting as I dart back to the room. As I come to a sliding halt, both hands gripping the doorway, I check inside to see if she's returned. The door is wide open and devoid of anyone, just like I left it. Immediately, I dial Penny. The phone rings once and I hang up. I dial again, this time letting the phone continue to ring. This is our official signal. No matter what either of us is doing, if the other calls, lets it ring once, then calls back, we know to drop whatever we're doing because it's an emergency.

By the forth ring, I hear a slight digital click and Penny's worried voice ask, "What's going on?"

While I dart to a different section of the hall, I explain I lost our new client when she went to the restroom. Finding no clues to our missing girl on this floor, I hit the stairs and head down a level.

"Can you access that not-so-legal GPS tracker you have?" I ask as I tear down the stairwell.

Penny doesn't mince words and replies, "My tablet's almost out of power and accessing it would drain it completely. Hold on, I'm calling Grant now. If he's at our apartment, I can walk him through using it on our bar top computer."

I'm now on the third floor, searching frantically for any clue as to where Beth could have gone. Coming across a snogging couple in the hallway, I grab their shoulders, physically breaking them apart, and ask if they've seen Beth. I go so far as to describe what she looks like and what she is wearing. Neither are a help, having been too preoccupied with each others lips.

"Okay! Okay!" I hear a pestered Grant say. Penny has obviously combined our two calls. "The program is up. Now what?"

"Free, you there?" Penny asks. "What's Beth's number?"

I read it back from memory. No way in the world could I explain how, considering I just learned it a few hours ago, but sometimes your mind surprises you when you need it most. Finally, stopping to take a breath, I look down another baby blue hall feeling a sense of déjà vu as I'm overwhelmed with dread.

"Grant, baby," I plead, hopelessness and panic threatening to consume me, "I really need you right now."

"I'm trying," He says at first in an annoyed voice. Realizing this request is coming from me and extremely urgent, he quickly changes his tone, "I mean... um... sorry... the map is coming up. Okay, um, it says she's... in the same place you are, Free."

Frantically, I check my pockets at first thinking someone slipped me her phone. I then realize this is not at all what Grant means.

"In the same building?" I ask.

"Yeah, I put both your numbers in so I could see both of you and guide you to her," he says in his innocently genius way.

"Grant, use the drag tool to highlight the building," Penny calls to her brother. "Then you should be able to manipulate the structure. It should become a wire frame you can rotate and zoom in on."

"Cool," Grant whispers, obviously finding exactly what his sister pointed to. "Okay, Free, she's really far below you."

Confused as to what that means, I at least know I'm going down. I run for the stairs, my arms slamming against the metallic handle as I charge through the door. My feet skip several steps and I tumble into the ugly, off-white stairwell wall on the landing below. Face first into the concrete, I may have just bruised my baby rolls.

"Grant," I plead, prying myself from the wall and staggering down the next flight. "I need more info."

"Right, well, you're going the right way," he says, doing his best to sound encouraging. "She's like another two floors below you."

Already on the second floor, my legs are functioning more effectively than my mind and I reach the lobby before I realize I'm out of floors.

"Grant, sweetie," I call. "Are you sure she's down one more floor?"

Also fighting off his own panic, Grant hastily replies, "I swear, she's one more floor below you. I mean, right below you too – like where you're standing. Can you blow a hole in the floor or something?"

Sometimes, he's adorably naïve.

The lobby of the dorm is linked to a rec room. The most brightly painted room in the building, pool tables line an upper deck of the room, nearest the windows, while a short set of stairs lead down into an area with couches, televisions, and a ping pong table. Directly to my right are several people working on old, outdated PC computers housed in cubbyholes. With such life inside, I head full steam toward the students, hoping someone can lead me further down this rabbit hole. Just as I open my mouth to shout across the room, I feel my body shift and slam into the archway leading inside. Everything is vibrating and I cannot maintain balance. Flesh to bone is trembling in an organized salvo of chaos. Holding onto the drywall archway for dear life, I realize it too is shaking with intensity. A few students call out and scamper under the pool tables and desks for safety. Pool cues drop from the walls in sharp clacks and a potted plant falls from a counter, shattering on the floor. My beating heart competes with my rattling teeth for who will deafen me first. An earthquake, without a doubt, was not what I needed right now. Got to love California.

A moment later and the vibration peters to a stall, causing students to wearily peek their heads out from under the tables in the hopes it is over. Noting the only shaking in the room stems from my own nervous system, I relinquish my grip from the wall.

"Good God," I say to Penny and Grant. "Did you feel that?"

"Yeah," Penny returns fairly calm. "There was a bit of a tremor here."

"A bit of a tremor?" I retort. "Damn thing nearly took me off my feet!"

Grant, hesitant of our sanity, adds, "What exactly are you guys talking about? I didn't feel a thing."

Ignoring my seemingly oblivious friends, I use the unsettling quake (and it was, regardless of what they say) as an excuse to ask my odd question.

Calling to one of the students who just left the confines of the pool table's belly, I ask, "Where's the basement?"

Dazed and still recovering his bearings, a young man answers, "You have to... you have to go through the laundry room."

He points a shaky finger toward a glass door at the end of the rec room. Rushing past the students, I toss the laundry room door open and pass inside. Another ugly, soft-white room, this one with several washer and dryer combinations lining the walls and half full laundry baskets scattered about. However, smack in the middle, breaking the line of machines, is a metal door with red letters etched across the top stating "Not an Exit." The door is sloppily painted the same shade of dull white as the rest of the room. An emergency evacuation map, slapped right in the middle of the door, advises victims to use another exit. By doing so, the map confirms this is the door I want, as the basement's exit is not likely intended for ground level emergencies. I turn the knob on the sloppily painted door to find it locked from the other side. Thankfully, there's no deadbolt and only the knob itself is locked.

Now is when my nonexistent lock picking skills step up to the plate. Turning round and round, my eyes search the tousled laundry room for my skeleton key. At first, I overlook my crimson ally, but a little voice in the back of my mind – the one that isn't fond of subtlety – grabs my head and refocuses my eyes on a little red darling affixed to a metal box behind me. Quickly, I remove the fire extinguisher from its case mounted in the wall and carry it to the locked door. Raising it above my head with both arms, I bring it crashing down with such intensity that, for the split second before it collides with the knob, I become afraid I might actually break a finger on impact. Metal on metal collide in a loud, hollow clang. And, while my lock picking tool is unfazed except for some chipped red paint, the doorknob to the basement has been cleanly removed and rolls to my feet on the floor.

I take a breath and hope to the great Buddha in the sky that I'm not making a mistake.

* * *

The cold grey walls of the basement are only comforted by the cob webs lining the corners. A few random street lights reflect through a meager number of slot windows resting just above ground level, while the remainder of the uninviting basement is lit by a scarce few hanging bulbs swaying from the rafters. I could have asked to explore a cheerier place. In fact, if I had to rank this basement versus the dingy alley I was in just last night, I think I prefer the alley. Hell, I prefer that horrific bar where I was groped over this place.

FREELANCER

The basement is equal parts machine room and warehouse. To my right, the buzzing electronic harmonies confirm it's the mechanical room. Directly in front of me, however, all I can see is a dark aisle lined with stacks of broken down, yet to be discarded rows of dormitory furniture. The blackness of the aisle seems to consume all light that touches it. Gazing into the distance, I feel as if I'm stepping through the basement's hollow, black pupil, while its iris – the brown stacks of furniture – closes in around me. Far in the distance, my only reprieve is a single glint of light – a single bulb - reflecting off the basement's eye, which has shifted its focus upon me. I shudder at the thought.

The humming mechanizations of the basement's lesser half make it impossible for me to hear what may lie ahead, but I trudge forward regardless. I cannot let Beth down. I will not.

Crossing stack after stack of furniture, my uneasy mind warns anyone or anything could leap out at a moment's notice. However, it is my uneasy heart that pushes me forward, reminding me Beth is our responsibility... and that I'm still carrying my "lock pick" should trouble charge out.

Nearing the single bulb, I gain an ounce of relief when I can finally see my surroundings as more than shadow and silhouette. But my ease is ill-earned and unnecessary.

The bulb before me sways ever so slightly.

As if standing on the train tracks before a locomotive, the ground quakes once more. I grab hold of a stack of broken down bunk beds, in equal parts to steady myself and equal parts to ensure they do not crash down upon me. This tremor, an aftershock of the last, is much milder. Yet, as the wood and I maintain a shared vibration, I note a few of the smaller pieces of furniture falling with loud clacks into the open aisle. The quake subsiding, I can only wonder: If such a minor tremor littered the aisle, then the major quake from earlier definitely should have too. That is, unless, someone else has been through here lately and cleared themselves a path.

Piercing the white noise of the basement, I hear a loud whimper and sharp, female scream. Beth's alive! However, the shriek is silenced so quickly, I can all but picture the stalker's gnarly hand angrily clasping its palm over her mouth.

Charging to a nearby intersection, I stop, realizing I have no idea which way to turn in this maze of misfit furniture. To my front is utter and complete darkness. To my right, however, I see another intersection about halfway down the aisle and an odd, bluish glow faintly ringing from it. Since becoming a Freelancer, I've had to rely on my instincts and danger magnet working in unison to guide me where I need to be. So far, I've had good fortune. I do not want this to be the day they falter.

Like a moth to flame, I dart for the blue glow and hope the mechanical room's noise drowns my approaching footsteps. Slowing down as I reach the edge of the aisle, I peek my head around to survey what evils may lurk there.

My eyes go glassy and the deathly grip of fear wraps its boney fingers around my throat. I'm petrified yet angered beyond words at the depravity I witness.

I'm already too late.

A man in a white cloak with a red fitted hood holds another of those white daggers well above his head. Blood drips upon him as if some sort of sickly baptismal. Above is a strange blue glowing light. The light's intensity against the darkness prevents me from making out just what it is, but the eeriness of the glow makes me wonder, if only for a second, if it's not the victim's very soul hovering above the corpse.

The body... the man... is in his forties with graying hair and was, before his shirt was ripped open, wearing a tweed jacket. As the sickly stalker, now turned murderer, drains the man's red, life-giving source into some sort of chalice, I hear the faint whimper of a girl. Looking beyond the glowing orb, I can vaguely make out Beth. She's struggling against something or someone. It's impossible to tell if there's a captor's hand covering her mouth or bindings holding her still. At any rate, I'm out of time. The murderous figure stands from the drained corpse. A goblet of blood in one hand and the white blade in the other, he skulks toward Beth.

I might get us both killed, but I can't just stand here. Without enough time to curse myself for not submitting my gun permit all those weeks ago... or... I guess I just did... I have maybe one chance at this.

Lunging from shadow, I raise my heavy, iron, highly pressurized weapon above my head, planning to bring it down upon the monster before me and to knock his knob off just as I had the basement door.

"Behind you!" I hear a voice near Beth warn.

50

FREELANCER

As I enter their blue, glowing field of vision, my violent intent obvious, the murdering cloaked figure attempts to turn my way. Both of us are sent reeling as another tremor strikes, throwing my aim and sending my extinguisher crashing into the murderer's chest. He tumbles to the ground, his goblet of blood tossed into the air. Meanwhile, my body rolls into Beth and her captor behind - the cup's sickly contents showering upon all three of us. Beth, her captor, and I are wrapped in a distorted mess of enemy and savior. The earth shaking moment stirs the captor from below me. Now that I can see him (and from his voice I can only assume this person is male), I can see he's wearing a violet and silver outfit complete with silver chest armor and a silver, fanged mask. I feel him throw my arm from his torso and push his way from below Beth. Slipping and sliding on the filth they wrought on the floor, he stumbles to his fallen friend and drags the murderer to his feet.

"It's done! It's done!" the captor says with a little more fear in his voice than I expected. "We have to go! Now!"

His cloaked, murderous friend uneasily stands from the trembling ground and surveys the bloody, tangled mess that is Beth and her would-be hero. The murderer's face obscured by a low-hanging hood, satisfied with the horrific results, heads for the safety of darkness, companion in tow.

But, just before disappearing completely, the murderous figure stops, turns to us, and says in a female, prideful voice, "You are free now."

And with those ominous words, the pair disappears into the shadows. As if the earth had been shaking out of fear at their presence, the quake finally ends. However, I could hardly tell it was over, as the girl below me sobs with such intensity her body is vibrating my own. A good chunk of me wants to chase these evil bastards down, but I know I can't. I came here to save Beth. This is where I'm supposed to be.

Cradling the frightened girl, I say, "They're gone. They're gone. It's okay. It's okay." I utter these words completely oblivious to how absurd they truly are. Beth is quick to enlighten me.

"Okay? Okay!" she stammers through her tears in disbelief. "It'll never be okay! They killed him! Those freakin' monsters! They murdered my father!" Angry, she lightly punches my chest in grief, just before clinging to it for support.

I now wonder. Did I truly save Beth? Or, is she now damned for a lifetime having witnessed this?

Chapter 5
Don't Talk to Me this Early

"You know," Dust begins in my ear, "I could kill you for last night."

"Just what a girl wants to hear while in bed," I say into my phone.

Thankfully, this time I made it all the way to my bedroom before collapsing into an exhausted mess. Long ago, I'd blacked out my window with the thickest, darkest curtains man had ever devised. Nary a ray of morning light encroaches on my darkened cave. Hurting, just like the day before, I've come to expect it during my Freelancing. The physical aspect of it all isn't what causes my exhaustion, it's the intensity. Once the adrenaline runs dry and my body has time to relax, I deflate into a rubbery heap.

Thus, this morning, I've yet to drag myself out of bed. Wearing an old t-shirt and my undies, I clutch the phone next to me and roll over, cocooning myself in the white, cottony confines of my overstuffed comforter. I was speaking with police, Dust included, until about 2 a.m. Beth was there for much of it but was eventually taken to the station where her mother awaited. I felt so horrible for the girl and guilty by measure. Somehow, I blamed myself, as if the danger magnet I carried somehow drew the threat to her. I know this to be a lie, but it feels so true. I should thank Ketchum with the back of my hand for planting this seed – for making me feel responsible for someone's death.

The police had found no sign of the murderers and no witnesses. The most they'd recovered was the victim's car in a nearby parking lot, but the vehicle had yet to yield any clues. Beth's father, considered the foremost expert in Theological Studies, had been giving a guest lecture at the university yesterday. The current working theory is he'd been abducted shortly after speaking. He was sedated, according to the toxicology report Dust just read to me, and snuck through the machine room door leading from the outside.

Dust and I believe this meant the murderers were on campus for hours. One of them likely attended the lecture, while the other waited for Beth to be alone. This also meant a couple of other things: 1) Someone had to have seen them on campus, and 2) Had I not left Beth alone, we might have prevented at least some of this.

In the end, they had no idea who the murderers were, how they accessed the girl's father, or what that blue glowing light was.

"Any luck on the dagger?" I ask Dust in my sleepy state.

How he's up and perky at 10 a.m. when he was with me until two o'clock I have no idea.

"Pfft – I called every source we have to figure out the symbols on that thing," he tells me. "I even called my Voodoo Grandma in New Orleans to see if she recognized them, but nobody has a clue what they are."

That's not very reassuring.

"You call her your *Voodoo Grandma*?" I ask, wondering if he's making things up. "That's not very PC of you."

"No," he corrects. "She calls herself my Voodoo Grandma. I'm just doing what I'm told."

One of these days, I'll figure out his insanely branched family tree.

"We have been able to determine one thing since yesterday," he adds. "It's not technically a bone knife that almost skewered you. The thing looks like bone or ivory, but it's actually made of something else. Techs aren't sure what yet. It's not common whatever it is."

"So," I add to the conversation, "It's a fake bone knife."

"I'd say that's accurate," Dust confirms with a smile in his voice. "And our other stalker, Stephen, has completely shut down. I tried interrogating him after the murder, but that was a mistake. He's already got some high-priced lawyer defending him, not letting him say a word."

Good news is in short supply today.

"Ugh," I say eloquently. "Don't call me again until you can make me happy."

"That's a tall order," Dust jokes. "Just get some rest. This has gotten much more serious than either of us expected, so I'd rather you bow out of this one. Let us do our jobs and I'll let you know if you can help."

Wait... did he just tell me to quit? Or, worse yet, did he indirectly fire me for Beth? At any rate, like that will happen. He should know better.

"Alright," I say noncommittally. "I guess just keep me posted."

JEREMY JAYNES

Dust and I wrap up our overly joyful conversation and I hit "end" on my phone. Tossing the small device on my nightstand, I wonder what other equally glorious news will greet me once I leave my room. Knowing I can't stay here all day (though I want to), I unwrap my bundled self and throw both legs over the side of the mattress. Instead of landing on the floor, the pads of my feet meet the disheveled remains of my red cocktail dress. Turning an eye to the rest of my room, I realize hardly an inch isn't covered by one of my many pieces of clothing. The thought of cleaning up is utterly depressing, so I squash it right away. Instead, I think I'll shower, but after coffee of course. Slipping off my t-shirt and underwear, I throw a robe on my naked caboose and run full steam... well, maybe half steam... or a quarter... I run ten percent steam into my day.

Opening the door, daylight ricochets off our white hallway walls to blast me in the face. As my bare feet begrudgingly carry me down the hall, I can hear thuds and grunts mixed with voices faintly ringing from our living room. At first as I enter the room, I fear we have been, in fact, invaded by ogres. There they stand, in some magic window, right above my living room floor. Thankfully, my mind is entirely too tired to care, so instead of panicking, I watch in puzzlement. My eyes adjusting to the scene, I realize an unconcerned Grant is sitting mere feet from them and the green and gray creatures seem to be hovering two feet above the floor. Thus, my sharp as a mallet mind concludes this must be a video game. When I see a white knight stab one of the ogres to death, blood spouting from its wounds like a geyser, and yet Grant and my white rug are not painted a new burgundy hue, my mind is satisfied with this conclusion. I continue shuffling and make my way to the coffee pot. Thankfully, my Penny loves me and has left it full. But, instead of the sweet smell of my caffeinated lover, once I near the sink I'm punched in the face with the foulest aroma. Damn it. I forgot to take the trash out like Penny asked. Oh well, what's a few more minutes. It can wait until after wake-up-juice.

Just as I pick up the pot, ready to enjoy its flavorful contents, Grant calls out to me, "I turned off the coffee. I did it to save you guys' electricity."

He says this as though it's a good thing.

From the television I hear, "Who are you talking to?"

"Don't' worry about it," Grant defends. "Just keep casting spells." He's obviously playing online, and instead of wearing the headset we've asked him to use repeatedly, he's utilizing the voice option over the console. If I wasn't so tired, I'd chastise him for the twelfth time over this.

I click the "on" switch to the coffee pot so it now glows in a glorious green, and shuffle my weary head to the counter behind me where I collapse onto a stool. Laying my head on the black top, I watch as Grant's white knight takes out an ivory white sword and begins fending off what seem to be tiny lizards or dragons. Hell, my eyes are so fuzzy right now, they could be leprechauns riding unicorns for all I know.

"Morning, Sunshine!" Penny says all cheerful and awake as she enters the room. She practically bounces across the hardwood floor. There's a spring in her step and a smile on her face.

I hate her.

"You didn't take the trash out," she lightly chastises, "But I'm sure you'll take care of that sometime today."

Now, I hate her more just for being glib.

"I've got class in a bit," she advises, "Do you have time for me to tell you what I found out?"

I mumble something inaudible. It might have been something distasteful about a part of her anatomy. I really don't know.

"Good," she says pulling up a stool opposite me.

With a swipe of her hand, she illuminates the bar top computer. Virtual keys display below her, while several files fall in categorical lines only she could ever understand. I continue watching Grant's enchanting game over her shoulder. The leprechaun unicorns have merged into some giant dragon. And, while an armored wizard protects a girl imprisoned in... I can't tell what that is... well, whatever it is, she can't move... so while the wizard protects her, Grant's knight is trying to slay the beast. I have to admit, it does look pretty fun. Personally, I typically prefer my games with more guns and copious amounts of gore. It's just how I was raised. But still, his game's fun too. If I can't figure out any leads today, this might be how I spend my depressed, failure of an existence this afternoon.

"So, I went ahead and looked into that connection between Katie and the first stalker, Stephen Hill," she tells me, while flipping through virtual files. I give her a grunt of curiosity in reply. I've yet to have coffee. We don't have words before coffee. Dust got a free pass because we were in bed.

"I"... I meant "I"... "I" was in bed. He was at the office, while I was in bed. "We" were on the phone. Not the both of us... in bed...

Shutting up now.

"Turns out Katie and Stephen went to this very exclusive private school together called..." Penny scrolls through a document on the bar top, searching for the name. "... called Moreland Academy. I also found out from Katie's social network accounts – accounts I did not hack into at all – that Stephen had been sending her messages repeatedly. They finally stopped about a month ago. Of course, none of them mentioned abducting her, but still."

That little bomb prompts my decaffeinated vocal chords into action.

"Katie never mentioned that when I interviewed her," I say somewhat suspiciously. As with any client, I have to question them at the start of a case. Katie was no different. Well, no different except it was her father answering most of the questions as Katie was too busy getting ready for our big night out, which coincidentally almost got us both killed.

Penny, just as suspicious but with a dash more sarcasm, replies, "No, no she did not mention this. And you'd think that would be a glaring red flag if you have a stalker."

Thinking out loud, I say, "Unless you were friends, so it was normal... Dust mentioned they knew each other."

I turn back to Grant's game. He's slayed the dragon by piercing the monster's heart with his white sword. The beast's blood oozes out onto the cave-like floor, while the wizard begins swirling some glowing mystical spell above them.

Penny calls to her brother, "Grant, we're leaving in ten."

Aggravated to be disturbed during this delicate ritual, Grant begrudgingly replies, "Okay!"

"Dude, who do you keep talking to?" a voice says from the TV.

Grant, enthralled by the game's goings on, replies, "I'm at my sister and Free's. I have to go in a few."

"Ohhhh," another voice says in a derisive tone. "You're at Free's, huh?"

"Dude...shut up," Grant nervously presents in his concise argument. "I'm not on headset."

"Have you seen her underwear today?" another voice chimes in.

"Dude," Grant says, grinding his teeth in embarrassment, "I'm not on headset. Knock it off."

I blow the comment off as adolescent boys being, well, *boys*. Instead, I shuffle off to the coffee pot, hoping it's warm by now. I'm half way to my brewed love when something sticks in the back of my mind. A notion – a clue – is clawing its way to the surface and trying to switch on the proverbial light bulb over my head. Changing trajectory, I head to my purse on the counter. Opening it, I find Ms. Sullivan's card staring up at me. The card reads:

Doctor Lauren Sullivan, PhD, MD
Senior Counselor
Moreland Academy

Oh, this cannot be a coincidence.

"Penny," I say to my friend who has turned all her attention toward the computer. "Where did Beth go to school?"

My Gal Friday, swiftly catching up to the same page, does a quick online search. The look on her face tells me as much as I need to know.

"Huh," she replies in ever the sarcastic tone. "Would you look at that? Beth also attended Moreland Academy."

We trade wry looks, signaling we both realize we're on to something. Lingering just a moment longer, I turn from my friend, my spirit elevated now that we have a lead, and head toward the coffee.

Just as I'm lifting the pot I hear from the television, "So, what color are they?"

"Guys, seriously," Grant chastises in a hushed tone. "Don't talk about her like that."

I should be pissed that he's talking about me to his friends, but I honestly feel more embarrassed for the poor guy. And he is trying to protect me in his meek little way. Unfortunately, the boys are only saying these things because they know it's getting to him. I only let it go because he needs to learn how to have a thicker shell. You can't let every bad word or annoying jibe get to you.

"Are you kidding?" an even more aggressive kid adds. "Grant, talk nice to her. Maybe she'll show all of us!"

"Guys, stop talking about her like that," he orders, his embarrassment eclipsing his anger.

"Yeah, Grant," another of the boys adds. "Why don't you ask her what color her panties are? Maybe you'll get lucky and we'll all get to see. Heck, it's probably the only way you'll ever see a girl in her underwear, anyway."

The honest fun of friendly jibes has grown into something more sinister. These boys smell blood. They pounce on Grant like a cackling group of hyenas, having a good laugh at his expense.

I am not.

"Yeah," grating voice number three says, "Tell her you're a virgin. Maybe that will help!"

I put the coffee pot down. Having gone from embarrassed for him to downright pissed off, I storm toward the living room. At this point, the boys have added video chat to their link so they can see Grant as well as hear him. Their tiny, beady little faces sit in the four corners of the screen. Storming to the couch, my robe billows behind me, encouraging my hand to clasp the cloth belt so it does not unfurl. As I do, a devious, menacing, would-make-my-mother-blush idea forms. Actually, I take that back. Mother would completely approve. I keep the robe tight, but expose just a crevice of skin up my chest - nothing more than a low-cut neckline, but enough for fifteen year old boys. Arriving at the couch, I rip the controller out of Grant's hands. I pull up the game menu and switch the audio and video so it can capture me as well as Grant.

Calling into the console I say, "If any one of you sausage-less losers thinks you've got more of a shot at seeing what's under this robe than Grant," I poke a leg out just for icing, "and you are seriously deluding yourselves."

Grant rears back on the couch, confused as to what he's witnessing. The pack of snarky animals he calls his "friends" quiet down immediately. A couple of their jaws fall open, and their eyes widen in awed bewilderment.

"And another thing," I add with such a gale force, even Penny has taken a keen interest. "Everything he told you about me is true." (At least, I hope so.) "But you were wrong about a couple things! Grant's not a virgin ... and I'm not wearing any underwear."

58

FREELANCER

Just as I pull the cord on my robe, I flick the game console's menu to "Save/Shutdown." Quickly, I clasp my robe, ensuring it never opens. However, the boys, having seen the gesture before the screen went black, will believe it did. I toss the remote back to Grant and re-tie my cloth belt. The young man's fawning eyes are full of fear, adoration, and a great deal of sexual attraction.

Ew.

"Just so we're clear," I add while tightening my belt further, "You will NOT be finding out what's under this robe."

With the comprehensive skills of a deer in headlights, he nods his shaggy head. At this point, I'm fairly certain he's become frozen in time – roughly thirty seconds ago by my calculations – so I could have told him I planned to cannibalize his sister and gotten the same reaction.

I make my way back to the kitchen where my coffee awaits. Scooping up my trusty mug just before scooping up my trustier pot, I pour a savory glass. As I take a whiff of the heavenly delight, I note Penny's sardonic gaze, which tells me I too probably need to work on my tougher shell. I decidedly pull back to the counter and join her.

"My parents will have him in therapy for years because of you," she says under her breath, then continues aloud, "So, where are you going first today?"

"Probably Katie's," I say, just before sipping from my cup. "Will hit Morewood Academy after."

"Moreland Academy," Penny corrects. Then, sarcastically adds, "Morewood Academy is where you just sent my brother."

Two good sips of coffee go by before I get the joke. Once I do, I turn a little red. I don't believe I need to apologize, do I? He'll have the best reputation ever thanks to me. Legends will be spun. Bards will sing tales. Orators will orate of Grant's ability to woo an older woman.

Legends, bards, and orators? My mind is still stuck in his game. I really do need to wake up... or play that game. It really looked cool.

"So what's the costume for today, then?" Penny asks of my indecisive wardrobe choices.

Contemplating this over another sip, I realize this will be tricky. I have to consider I'm stopping by Katie's, a private high school, and possibly the police station.

"I'll probably avoid my Katie Protector stuff and go straight for hot dick," I say without thinking.

Penny, whom I can rarely rattle, pushes back from the bar computer and drops her jaw before saying, "You'll what?"

Grant, having just recovered from my antics, was taking a drink of milk when I replied. Upon hearing my words, he simultaneously gasps and swallows, nearly drowning in his two percent. The coughing fit is so horrendous, he turns red and falls across the couch trying to recover. I wonder if he might throw up.

"Detective!" I correct. "I meant *hot detective*! My persona... Hot Private Detective. Not... not something else."

Penny turns around to make sure her brother survives his intolerant lactose state. I can hear the wheezing of his breath and an involuntary spasm as he tries to suppress the coughing. Feeling his sister's gaze, Grant shoots us a thumbs up from behind the couch, indicating he'll live.

"Okay, maybe I should change the name of that persona to *sexy cop*," I add.

Penny, turning back to me, advises, "Not unless you're playing a stripper today. In which case, it would explain a lot about you."

"Right," I say with a little more embarrassment kicking in. I really have a habit of making an ass of myself in front of Penny. More to myself than anyone, I add, "This is why I don't talk to people before coffee."

"How about we rename it *Cute P.I.* and call it a day," Penny says, saving me from my mind's further deranged ramblings.

"Yes, well, I want to be taken seriously," I continue, realizing how foolhardy that sounds after the last five minutes, "but still have an advantage over any men I run into. Katie's dad seemed into me, so Cute P.I. ... the persona formerly known as Sexy Private Detective...

"And Hot Dick," Penny corrects derisively.

Pausing for lack of embarrassed breath, I finish, "...Cute P.I. could play."

Honestly, I don't want people to think I use sexuality to get what I want. That's not the case at all. I just use my personas to throw people off balance. Of course, I may occasionally use men's hormones (and sometimes women's) to reveal facts about a case or allow me to do things that I might not get to if I was dressed like a nun instead. But those are just some of my weapons. It's all about reading the situation and knowing what will be most effective. I've learned the way I dress and how I present myself factor in much of the time.

FREELANCER

Finishing my coffee, I pull myself from the stool and head back for another cup. My mind and body are finally feeling a little more recharged. I'd say we're finally at half steam.

"Free," Penny begins while I'm refreshing my glass. "Can I suggest something?"

I'm mid pour when I say, "Sure? What?"

"If you want to be seen as a professional today," she says in a tone so serious, it tells me she's not, "You might want to consider putting on some underwear."

Replacing the coffee pot, while simultaneously hiding my embarrassment, I reply, "Noted."

Chapter 6
I'll take the Orc. You get the Wizard.

The taxi pulls away from the Worthington estate as I unbutton the top button of my blouse. "Cute P.I." will be played today by Elizabeth Freeman. She sports a nice white top, red overcoat, and just-long-enough-to-be-professional but short-enough-to-be-sexy black skirt with underwear firmly affixed below, as suggested by her best friend. Adjusting my skirt slightly, I take in the home before me.

A palace of brick and mortar laid on a foundation of money, Mr. Worthington does well for himself. The front of the house is a muted yellow, while the molding around the door and tall pillars before it are a fine white like the whipped crème on their lemon meringue. I stand near a small fountain adorning the center of the circular drive. As I approach the house, taking heed of the stone porch with nary a crack, the housekeeper, Ms. Sheldon or "Candace" if I remember correctly, opens the door to greet me. She's an older woman, probably in her early sixties, short and plump just like you'd expect in a well-loved grandmother.

"Ms. Freeman," She says. "It's so good to see you. Mr. Worthington isn't at home, but Katie is expecting you on the swim deck."

Of course she is.

"Oh," I say in averted horror, "And here I didn't bring a swim suit."

Thank God. The last thing I want to hear is a snide remark from Katie on how my boobs are so last year.

"Actually," Ms. Sheldon replies. "Katie asked me to find you a suit when you arrived."

Did I say averted horror? No, no this just seems to be head-on horror. Honestly, I don't really have much of an opinion on Katie. I don't know her well enough to form one. She's younger than me, and we didn't exactly bond over her near-kidnapping. Even when we got our hair done together, they whisked her off to another section of the building, so we hadn't spoke much. But, from what I've seen, she seems much less mature than I am and very materialistic and shallow – not the type of person with which I typically associate. Reading the dismay in my eyes, the kindly housekeeper seems to take pity.

Candice adds, "Thankfully, I've been unable to find a swimsuit that would fit you."

Some blood returns to my cheeks and I pat the kindly woman on the shoulder.

"Ms. Sheldon," I tell her. "You are officially on my Christmas Card list."

The older housekeeper shows me through the kitchen where every appliance is made of the new, white Plexi-Clean material. The pearl-like substance has been all the rage, but just a little too expensive for every home to flaunt. Hardly an inch of the room doesn't gleam of pearl or ivory. The selling point for the product is the fact that, regardless the wear and tear, they are certified to remain a vibrant white for a lifetime.

"I don't think I've seen this much Plexi in one place," I tell Ms. Sheldon.

Stopping to survey the kitchen proudly, she replies, "That's because you're standing in the kitchen of the man who made it possible."

Dumbfounded this did not come up in our background check, I ask, "Mr. Worthington invented Plexi?"

Laughing, Ms. Sheldon replies, "No, no! Not at all, but he fixed the computer that did. Mr. Worthington built Sensation Limited – the computer software company." My ignorance of the significance is apparent. "He made that popular game, Fantasy War. But more importantly, he made the engine that goes into the game."

I remember back to the meeting with Penny – another early morning session where she was trying to talk to me while I was having coffee. Thankfully, the night before I had not been Freelancing; therefore, I was moderately awake. Penny mentioned Worthington was a famous computer guy who invented some "engine." Not wanting to feel stupid at the time, I didn't ask what that meant.

Realizing I still don't know what she's talking about, Ms. Sheldon adds, "Picture an engine as what drives a game just like your car. Way more complex than I could ever explain, but those people over at Able Corp. went nuts for it. Mr. Worthington's invention helped them make Plexi. Now, we get as much Plexi product as anyone could ever want."

I'm still a little fuzzy on this whole engine thing, but I think I have the gist.

"In case I need to speak with him," I ask Ms. Sheldon, "Do you know when Mr. Worthington will be home?"

"Oh, I really have no idea," she says using her finger to wipe a smudge from the pristine white counter. "Mr. Sheldon doesn't keep a set schedule. We don't see him for what seems like days at a time."

For me, a girl who grew up without her father, that seems horrible. However, Katie is a few years younger and probably still trying to wrestle control of her own perceived freedoms from her dad. I have to admit, when I was sixteen, I loved it when Mom was away. Of course, now I actually miss the comfort of her company most of the time.

I step to the door leading to the deck and spy Katie outside. She's sunbathing across the pool, closest to their ten foot fence, and lying so she faces the door, making sure no one is able to sneak up on her. Noting she is alone, I realize the private security team Mr. Worthington had hired is no longer present. Considering the threat had been neutralized, he must have dismissed them. Most rich people don't keep armed guards around unless they have a reason. In my short experience, millionaires are just people like you and me but with bigger bank accounts and nicer cars.

"So, how is Katie holding up since the other night?" I ask. "Is she handling it okay?"

A pang of concern crosses Ms. Sheldon's face, and she rings her hands – an obvious tell she does not consciously seek to avoid. Her concern informs me, while she may be paid to live here, she considers this family hers all the same.

"I thought my Katie was stronger than this," the housekeeper advises. "She's grown up in a..." Ms. Sheldon stops herself as if she's about to reveal too much. "She's been raised to be strong – to be as strong as her mother before her. But these last couple of nights... well, I just hope she's able to get back to normal soon."

FREELANCER

I understand completely. Most victims suffer nightmares for weeks after any kind of traumatic event. I still have them from time to time, and I've lived a lifetime of trauma. Katie, while she may have a superficial shell, is still just as soft and breakable as any of us on the inside.

"Ms. Freeman," Candace asks. "Please just keep in mind, my Katie – she's a lot like her father was when he was younger. She's not always great with people, and her own intellect seems to distract her sometimes. It can get confused with... other things. So please be patient."

I'm trying to understand her meaning but don't really comprehend what she's getting at. When I first met Ms. Sheldon, right before I met Katie, she said something similar but I didn't get it then either. Instead of questioning her meaning, I decide to placate the woman.

"I will," I advise with insincere assurance.

Opening the door to the pool, I step outside. The swim deck is about as lovely as any part of this grand home. The pool is Olympic-sized with a floating bar to one side and numerous umbrella chairs surrounding. Realizing my heels will not due on the deck, I remove them to feel the surprisingly smooth, rocky surface below. The deck is composed of what looks like multiple stones inlaid into cement, but a fine glaze has been poured over top to ensure one's bare feet pleasantly grip an even surface. Following the shoes, I remove my coat and throw it over my arm. I don't want to sunbathe, but it is a nice summer day and I could use a little color.

Nightmares or not, I can already tell Katie's vanity is intact. Even from this distance I can see Katie's tiny white bikini would be deemed inappropriate on most beaches. Heck, even if you paid me a king's ransom and promised to bail me out after I was arrested for indecent exposure, I still wouldn't wear that thing. How one could strut around in something so revealing is beyond me. Of course, I try to ignore the nagging part of my brain that says, "Yeah, but what if you had to wear it for a Freelancing case?" Let's just hope that's one persona I never have to take on.

Approaching the girl, I note the plexi-white sunglasses hide her eyes, while matching white earbuds deafen her with music, distracting from my approach. However, once I'm within a few paces, as if stirred from slumber, Katie shakes her head and sits up stiff as a board. With a quick yank, she strips out her earbuds and launches from her chair like a child greeting a favorite grandparent.

"Free!" she shouts.

65

Like a missile of good tidings, the girl hones in on me. I honestly don't know what to do.

Her arms wrap around me in the biggest hug the tiny girl can muster, and she says in a nearly out of breath machine gun fire of words, "I'm so happy to see you! Candace told me you were coming today! I hope you can stay awhile! I've got it all planned out! We'll have a blast!"

You'd think I was her long lost best friend.

Awkwardly patting the girl on the back, I return the hug with such stiff arms it's as if my joints have petrified. Until now, the notion hadn't occurred to me the events of the other night might have had a discernable impact on the girl. She cradles me for an obscenely long time before I finally wrestle myself from her grip.

"I'm glad to see you're okay," I say genuinely, moving myself to arm's length. "So how are –?"

"You aren't wearing a swimsuit!" She cuts off as though I'm on fire. "I told Candace to give you one! Why aren't you wearing one?"

The more she speaks and the more I see of her (her inappropriate swimsuit not withstanding) the more I can see she's been damaged both internally and externally. A few bruises are noticeable on her arms and stomach, while a fairly bad scrape adorns her knee. Thankfully, my wake-up slaps had not left marks on her already pretty face. The other night must haunt her with each ache or pain. In all though, her exterior damage was pretty minimal all things considered.

"I'm sorry, Katie," I apologize to the animated girl. "I can only stay for a little bit."

I'm not kidding when I say tears form in her eyes, no less so than if I told the girl her favorite puppy had died.

"No – no – no – you can't..." she pleads. "You're supposed to stay, and we were going to hang out and have lunch and maybe watch a movie and have dinner."

Katie, a girl who could probably buy friends by the truckload, needs something – someone substantial to hold onto. This may be the exact type of girl I typically don't hang out with, but she's also a girl who needs a shoulder right now. And in reality, that's exactly why I started Freelancing. I'm such a sucker for wounded souls.

With a begrudging exhale of breath, I advise, "I guess I can stay for a little while."

* * *

Ms. Sheldon is a saint.

As I sit here sunning in the afternoon heat, beads of sweat running down my skin, and a much calmer Katie keeping me company, I at least feel the tiniest bit of modesty. Upon agreeing to stay with Katie, the kindly old woman went to fetch a swimsuit. When she returned with a couple of suits she had obviously picked up for guests, Katie was unimpressed. The woman had returned with a black one-piece with ruffles and a full bottom skirt, looking like something my dead grandmother would wear, and a second, more tasteful red and black two-piece which I preferred. However, neither was sufficient for my former client, and Katie took off like a shot in the dark to find something more suitable for my figure.

Actually, I think she put it as, "You're bod will look so amped!"

Looking at the "Brazilian cut" swimsuit she returned with, which would rival her own in infamy, it wasn't my bod that was amped – it was my low self-esteem. Which, in all honestly, hiding behind personas typically keep my esteem issues at bay. I mean, whether I'm showing skin or dressing like a hobo, as long as I'm in a persona, I don't feel like it's me that's being judged. However, today, in this situation, I'm not so much "Cute P.I." as "Free the friend."

Analyzing the suit, my first thought was this girl was evil and solely wanted to embarrass me. There was no other explanation because there was no way on this green Earth I would wear something that skimpy next to a girl who looks like someone should be paying her to bend over a sports car.

That sounded better in my head.

I meant in a calendar or magazine... not... not paying her for something else...

Moving on.

Point is she's really pretty and I do not want a comparison thrown at me today. However, to satiate her incessant pleas, I took Katie's swimsuit and the red and black two-piece Ms. Sheldon brought, and told her I'd try both on.

It's not very nice to lie. I know, but the modest fib got me out of a very awkward situation.

However, when I returned wearing the red and black suit, I could finally see Katie's eagerness was not feigned. She was utterly and completely disappointed when she saw me in the other suit, as opposed to her jet black dental floss. She had sincerely wanted me to share in one of her things, to bond over common loved apparel, and I had shot her down like some stranger in her house, which, to my credit though, I practically am.

In her deflated, semi-pouting state, she went so far as to compliment my figure and say I'd look much better in the black suit than she ever did. According to her, the suit I was wearing was just not me and did nothing for my great figure. Honestly, as she spoke, I couldn't help but find her darling. At that point, with her lip all but turned out in disappointment, I told her when we got together again I'll wear the black one. Her little face turned pleased as punch when she noted I said when we get together *again*. As if I somehow made the girl's day, she turned positively buoyant and jumped right into the pool full of life and energy – things Ms. Sheldon alluded to as missing from the girl.

Taking stock of Katie, still in the pool but currently floating on a raft, I've had time to contemplate just what she's doing with me. I realize this isn't a new situation, and my ex-client's feelings right now are nothing you can build a friendship on. Heck, my Bad Penny and I are the best of friends because she never succumbed to it.

Thy beast be named "Hero Worship."

Not the ugliest of beasts, but it is one which must be tamed. Katie needs someone to hold her up right now, someone to prove there's greatness out there, and I'm it. Now, I don't mean this to sound conceited. I'm not. In fact, I think her adoration is undeserved. But no matter how hard I try, Katie won't see I'm a regular girl like her until she gets some distance from the other night. Then and only then, would we see if we could be real friends... not that I'm betting on it.

"Kate," I ask, "Did you know your stalk... I mean, Stephen? I heard he went to school with you."

I'd been trying to pose questions like this off and on all morning, peppering them into meaningless conversation. I could tell Katie's fragile frame of mind wouldn't be able to handle direct questioning, and an indirect approach, though taking longer, was working best. I'd already asked if she'd heard about Beth, and if the two of them were close in school.

With defensive sorrow she replied, "We used to be."

FREELANCER

Pondering my last question or fast asleep, the girl floats along in her airy tube for the longest time without so much as a word. Her eyes are hidden behind her dark, white-rimmed glasses, and she shows little movement. Finally, she scoops up the tiniest amount of water and drips it across her stomach, proving her tiny self is still with me.

"Yeah," she replies in a morbid, hollow tone. "But... but he was different then."

I press a little more.

"A nicer guy, a friend, completely dateable," I add with some understanding. "And not crazy to boot. I get it."

Katie almost laughs, but her trauma rings it dead.

"Stephen? Not at all!" She says with her lifeless laugh and a sad longing. "I mean, he was always a sweetheart, but he was such an unrepentant nerd. I kind of loved him for that, but... he was just one of those guys you could talk to about anything. You know? I never thought he'd..."

She lets her train of thought go, but I can't stop the subject while we're on it.

"So did you guys talk at all this summer – after graduation?" I ask with a sincere, naïve curiosity that should win me an Oscar.

"Yes and no," she tells me. "I'd hear from him every once in a while, but it was always weird. He'd write me these messages that were like half conversations. Nothing like, you know, I'm planning on kidnapping you. But still, I didn't understand them. Finally, when I didn't respond to some of his stuff, he just stopped trying."

This actually jives with the fact Penny found several messages from Stephen in Katie's social network account but found scarce few outbound messages to Stephen from Katie.

"He was such a harmless guy with a good heart," she says in retrospect. "Said he'd always protect me. Kind of feel like I should have protected him."

Katie, for all her outwardly material vanity, is more like me than I thought.

"Kate," I begin, "If you only knew how many times I've felt the same way." There's no lie here. Some of the people I've been closest to over the years turned out to be just more of my danger magnet at work. "So you couldn't see this coming from him?" It's a harsh question but has to be asked.

Katie shifts in her floating chair, signaling the discomfort she feels... Or that shoestring bikini finally rode into the wrong place.

69

"Like I said," she returns morbidly, "He always said he'd protect me. No way did I think that would involve kidnapping me."

We ponder our heavy hearts with the sun beating down and the sweat baptizing our fair skin. Well, my skin is fair. Katie looks as though she spends a great deal of time out here.

"Hey," Katie calls from her raft in the pool, suddenly alive with her hero-worship-induced energy. "You hungry? I was thinking of ordering a pizza and popping in this really cool video game I have." She stops short, feeling embarrassed. "Man, I hope you don't think I'm the biggest nerd, but have you heard of Fantasy War? Dad made it and it's so much fun!"

The awesome game I saw Grant playing! Yikes, he might be rubbing off on me if I'm this excited.

"I may have heard of it," I reply in contained enthusiasm.

Offering pizza, a cool video game, and complementing my figure? Suddenly my Bad Penny has competition for a new best friend.

* * *

Katie and I sit in her extravagant family room, wrapped in the finest violet robes my skin has ever had the privilege to touch. The room is set-up with an incredible sound system, eighty-eight inch HoloGraph television, and numerous amounts of fantasy swords, axes, and armor hanging from the walls or on pedestals around the room. Katie had started to explain what each and ever one of the weapons represented, but stopped short, embarrassed by all the fantasy knowledge her little head holds.

An open pizza box sits on the brass and copper coffee table in front of us with most of the delectable pieces gone or currently being consumed. We'd showered while waiting for the pizza, and ended up watching half a girly movie we'd both seen a dozen times while we ate. Now, we are finally ready to begin Fantasy War. I'm looking forward to this game way more than I should.

I can never tell Grant.

Katie goes over the basic controls in a very animated format. She explains you can use a controller or the motion sensors, but with two of us, it would be best to stick to controllers because she's accidentally smacked people while flailing her arms around. This causes me to agree with the controller option whole heartedly.

We spend the next two hours engaging in virtual swords and sorcery, laughing at how poorly I play and how much of a nerd she must be to play so well. My character's class, a Rogue, is a scrapper that flings herself across the battlefield, wielding two white blades with which to eviscerate her foes. The game allows for the player to scan themselves in – literally uploading a digital version of yourself into the game, which I did so immediately and placed my character in a leathery red dress with white cape and armor. Oh, the fun of seeing myself leap across the holographic landscape and impale a troll is boundless.

Oddly, while Katie plays this game often, her character is completely fictional. Instead of scanning her pretty face and perfect little princess body, she's chosen to play as a fictional Barbarian. A huge, lumbering brute of a male character, the complete opposite of her, he carries an axe as large as his own body and slices through his foes in gleeful carnage. For such a character to actually be a five foot nothing blonde is rather amusing, if not scary. As we raid another dungeon, seeking to liberate the damsel in distress, I remember Grant's friends playing with him and wonder if we should do the same.

Innocently, I ask, "Hey, do you have any other friends on here? Are we going to play with them?"

My Rogue is crashing down upon the head of a wizard, or "mage" as I've learned they are called, while I ask. And it's only by chance that I catch Katie's face in the corner of my eye. Though I did not mean to at all, the winded look and flushed checks tell me somehow I just sucker punched the girl. The whole room seems to grow darker and quieter as all light and sound is swallowed by her uncomfortable pain.

She attempts to play it off and without turning her eyes my way says, "No, my friends... I don't have ... no, we won't be."

As I look at the pained girl, trying not to stare, I have to wonder what occurred in her life to chase all her friends away. After a traumatic event like the other night, this girl needs all the love and support she can get, but she acts as though she's all alone.

Is it her personality? Her superficial ways? Her vanity? If so, I'm beginning to wonder if it's undeserved. Oddly, I find her superficial demeanor to be superficial in itself. She tends to play the part of spoiled rich girl, but her true identity remains to be seen. Or, maybe that's what I'm seeing now. Maybe she's just a girl – one who secretly likes sunning, eating pizza, and playing video games. But there is also another, more nagging concern. The possibility also remains maybe her lack of friends has nothing to do with her personality at all, and more to do with something she may have done to drive them away.

Chapter 7
Back to School

I walk through the hall of Moreland Academy, at once feeling as though I don't belong to such an elite educational institution and yet feeling very much the same nervous excitement that drove me through the halls of my own school. The floor shimmers with a fresh coat of wax, likely reapplied every evening, while the windows are so entirely spotless, they seem invisible. The walls are painted with a fresh coat of violet in certain sections, and a dull crème in others – the school colors. The combination is done so artfully, the color scheme is only accented by the fine hand carved crown molding gracing every doorway and seam. The janitor guides me down the hall which is filled with row after row of pristine lockers. School is out of session, summer classes over for the day, so only the echo of my heels and the soft step of his shoes bustle through the hall.

The kindly janitor leads me to Ms. Sullivan's finely crafted wood and glass door. In order to ensure I am not in the wrong place, her name has been carefully stenciled upon the frosted glass. How thoughtful.

I knock briskly just before opening the door without invitation. The office is large enough to accommodate a classroom full of kids. Bookshelves line the wall to the right with her various degrees hanging between them. A lavish leather couch is offset to the side, while a small table with matching chairs sits on the opposite. Her finely crafted desk rests at the far end of the room, positioned in front of a large window overlooking the schoolyard. From here, one could bear witness to a great many of the goings on between students. As I enter, Ms. Sullivan happens to be reaching for something sitting atop one of the filing cabinets flanking her magnificent window. Noting my intrusion, she stops fidgeting for the errant item and turns around.

Straightening her jacket and blouse, she appraises me before speaking, "I'm sorry, I didn't hear you knock at first."

"My fault," I explain. "I didn't give you a lot of time to answer." Actually, that was intentional. Throwing people out of their comfort zone gives me the advantage. Plus, barging into someone's inner sanctum – an intrusion like that gives me the best footing.

Studying me further, Ms. Sullivan assesses, "Too uncomfortable to be a student, but you seem awfully familiar. Have we met?"

Good guess.

"We met last night," I reply. "I'm Free, Beth's friend."

"Free!" She says, finally recognizing the girl who failed to keep her former student safe. "Oh, my goodness, dear! Are you alright? How is Beth holding up?"

Crap. I came here to ask the questions, but this lady seems genuine, so I don't want to completely ignore her. However, I've got to maintain some semblance of dominance over the conversation. Thankfully, my little Katie-vacation pulled my confidence meter out of the "mopey" category and into "ticked off." Now I just want to find out who's behind hurting these girls and their families. I cross the full length of the room to Ms. Sullivan's desk.

"I'm fine," I say in the best business-as-usual attitude I can muster. "Beth is doing about as well as expected, and that's why I'm here. Did Beth happen to explain to you what I do?"

Puzzled, Ms. Sullivan asks, "Do? What do you mean?"

Efficient and cool, I pull a business card from my coat. However, instead of handing it across her desk, her comfort zone, I walk around it, step to her, and then hand her my card. As she takes the small piece of cardboard, I expect her to take a small step back, signaling her discomfort at my close proximity. Instead, she takes a step forward so she's within inches of me, and I take the step back. She throws another appraising look at me just before turning to the card.

Moving away from the desk, I turn my back on her and head for the degrees on the wall. My first tactic being an utter failure, I figure I might as well read her credentials while she reads mine. Oddly, I expect her to begin speaking to me well before reaching her degrees, which are half way across the room. However, she does not, and I reach her framed diplomas in no time. Reading her credentials, I keep her in the corner of my eye, believing she watched me walk all the way over here, studying my every step.

Breaking the silence, I say, "You're a doctor, but Beth calls you 'Ms.' – why is that?"

Casually, in her same friendly demeanor, she replies, "I want my students to think of me as a teacher first and a doctor second. Actually, I'd like them to think of me as a friend first, but that's even more difficult since I am faculty. Regardless, if a student saw you walk in here today, they would think you came to see Ms. Sullivan – a teacher. However, if you came in here to see Doctor Sullivan, then without ill intent, the first thought to pop into someone's mind would be –."

I cut her off with, "There must be something wrong with me."

"Exactly," she replies. "And I've always wanted my students to feel safe coming here."

I look over her degrees further – Oxford, Yale, Johns Hopkins. She's very well educated. I'm severely out of my league and using these tactics aren't getting me anywhere. Noting my discomfort, Ms. Sullivan circles around her desk and makes her way to me. Her expensive heels clack their way across the hardwood floor until they reach the rug below me.

"So what exactly is a Freelancer," she asks curiously. "I've not heard the term in this context before."

Knowing whatever answer I give has to be honest, yet can't allow further ground, I advise, "A little bit of everything. I have a Private Investigator's license if that makes you feel better."

Guarded, controlling of the information given, yet a truthful answer – I deserve a cookie. Honestly, Dust made me get a license. He said it was the closest to legitimate as he could get me. Penny got us the rest of the way by getting us registered as a business.

Suspiciously, Ms. Sullivan asks, "Aren't you awfully young to be a Private Investigator? What would bring you to this type of work?"

"Besides all the fame and fortune it brings me?" I joke, deflecting the comment.

Ms. Sullivan isn't amused. In fact, she looks at me with the same concern in her eyes she flashed at Beth just last night. Right, deflection not going to work on a psychiatrist.

"Let's just say I've got a knack for sniffing out trouble," I answer honestly, then parry with, "Why did you become a teacher? You could obviously make a lot of greenbacks as a private shrink."

With a warm, reflective smile, she says, "The shortest answer is: I've always wanted to work with children – young adults. Moreland offered this... plus some of those *greenbacks* you seem fond of. So, instead of a few children coming to see me, I have a couple hundred."

What a nice statement. But, as I've learned from Dust, now is when I need to attack.

I barely let the heartfelt sentiment leave the air before I launch into, "So how well do you know Katie Worthington?"

Finally, I make Ms. Sullivan deflect.

"I thought you were here about Beth?" She asks, taken off guard.

"How do you know Katie?"

And my question is already answered. Ms. Sullivan knows her.

"Katie's one of my clients," I advise. "Just like Beth."

As I'm already standing near the couch, Ms. Sullivan holds her arm out gesturing for me to sit. I do so, while she adjusts her skirt and takes a seat in the chair across from me. When she crosses her legs, I can't help but stare at her magnificent shoes.

"Katie and Beth aren't your friends then?" she asks curiously.

Kind of an ugly question. I like them both just fine... well, maybe not Katie so much at first, but she's grown on me. But again, we barely know each other, so "friends..."

"I wouldn't say that exactly," I reply.

"Then what would you say?" Ms. Sullivan continues with her examination.

I swear, this woman's analytical gaze is somewhere between doctor running an experiment and skeptical mother. When I don't answer right away, she re-crosses her legs – right over left this time – and folds her hands in her lap, waiting for a reply. Pondering just how to keep this woman out of my head, I turn my attention back to those exquisite Marcus Nelly shoes on her feet. Like the snapping of fingers, my mind jumps back to memories of the police station yesterday. Dust and Ketchum are arguing about me, while I pretend to compose a text. A pair of lone Marcus Nelly pumps clack past – a pair of Marcus Nelly pumps coming from the lockup's visitors' area.

Ignoring her question entirely, I ask, "So how was your visit with Stephen Hill yesterday?"

I'll hand it to her, Ms. Sullivan isn't the least bit surprised by the question. In fact, she throws a pleased grin my way, as if she's proud of me for putting the pieces together.

"As good a visit as one can expect when your former student is locked up for kidnapping and assault," she says.

"So you know Stephen, Katie, and Beth," I continue. "Would you say you know them well?"

Finally, after all this verbal sparring, Ms. Sullivan looks uncomfortable. However, the glint in her eyes and clench of her jaw tells me I've not so much as hit a nerve, as run into some sort of wall.

"You aren't too bad at this. I can see you've done it before," she says somewhat relieved. Up until this point, she probably still thought of me as some girl playing detective. "But before we go any further I must point out that as a counselor in this school I cannot divulge any private information about my students."

Hmm, this could pose a problem.

"Even people who are no longer your students?" I more or less point out.

Ms. Sullivan gets quiet. She stands and walks her thousand dollar shoes to her thousands of dollars desk. Passing it by, the woman chooses to have a moment of reflection as she peers out the magnificent window.

"You must understand, Free," she advises. "The students at Moreland are the children of some very powerful men and women, so I must be careful of what I say and to whom I say it."

"But I'm here to help these girls," I all but demand. "Don't you want to help them too?"

Ms. Sullivan grows very quiet and her shoulders slump ever so slightly. I can see there is a ferocious tidal wave of information she's holding back with all of her might, and her levies are beginning to buckle. Unfortunately for me and the girls I'm protecting, she is a very strong willed woman. But she is also very kind.

"If I didn't want to help them," she tells me with a great deal of heart, "You would not still be here." She grows quiet again and does not continue. I take this as an opening to press further.

"So, did you know the girls from counseling?" I ask. "Or, were they just students at the school?"

As if fact checking something in her head, she pauses before answering, "I had seen them on a counseling basis, yes."

"Stephen too?" I continue.

Again, she pauses before answering, "Yes."

"I probably can't ask what they were seeing you about, can I?"

Ms. Sullivan laughs wearily and says, "You can ask but I can't answer."

Changing my position, I ask, "What about outside of your office – in school? Were they friends?"

The kindly, yet defensive psychiatrist gives me a wry smile as if she'd been waiting for me to get here. As she does, I realize I'm asking a general question that anyone could observe, meaning it doesn't fall under her confidentiality issues.

"Beth was a social butterfly in school," she tells me. "Walk down these halls, and you'll find pictures of her in all kinds of activities. Theater, dance, cheerleading..."

Cheerleading? Ugh, I may have Beth figured all wrong.

"So she was really well-liked," I finish for her. "What about Katie? Graduating at sixteen, she had to be the youngest person in her class. That had to cause problems."

Ms. Sullivan gives me a look that tells me she's once again fact checking the information she's about to divulge. Her face further warns my last comment tows the line of confidentiality a little too closely.

"I'd definitely call Beth popular. But Katie was not the youngest in her class," the woman answers. "Two of her classmates were younger by several years."

Realizing she didn't exactly answer my question, I ask, "So did you ever see Katie and Beth hanging out in social situations with Stephen? Were they friends?"

"Friends as you've already pointed out," Ms. Sullivan replies, "Is a relative term. I noted Katie and Beth were in several activities together, as well as attended several functions with one another for the longest time."

"*For the longest time*," I mimic. "This implies at some point it ended. Did you notice they were no longer talking or hanging out?"

Man, I've really got my cop on today. Dust would be so proud.

Carefully, Ms. Sullivan replies, "I happened to witness several instances of Katie saying hello to Beth in the hall, but Beth not responding."

I can't say that's a lot to go on. How many girls did that to me in High School?

"What about Stephen?" I press. "Was he friends with Katie and Beth? Did they seem to have a falling out too?"

"Hmm, well, for clarification," she begins, "*From what I witnessed in the halls*, Beth hardly gave Stephen and his friends the time of day, but Katie was always very friendly to them, waving hello and greeting them if they passed."

"Wait," I intrude. "Katie? Stuck-up, conceded, Katie Worthington? The girl who dresses like a rich tramp and talks like a spokesmodel?"

Ms. Sullivan chuckles and says, "She's got you fooled too then... All I can say is, Katie seems to... in public... dress a certain way and put out this quality about herself... yet, she was always friendly to Stephen and his group, though they were not nearly as socially accepted as her."

Katie's a secret nerd! That totally fits with what I saw earlier. Unfortunately though, it sounds like my girl, Beth, might have been a little stuck-up.

"So, did Stephen and the girls have any activities together?" I continue. "I'm trying to understand how he knew Beth, outside of passing her in the halls."

"I'm not aware of any school activities they were involved in together," Ms. Sullivan says cryptically. "Well, not any activities that would not breach confidentiality anyway." Her eyes are practically boring into my very soul as she utters those last words. She's telling me something without actually telling me. Whatever this activity is she can't discuss, is exactly what I need to know about.

"If I was you," Ms. Sullivan continues, "I'd ask Katie or Beth."

"You know, Ms. Sullivan," I return, thanking her with my eyes as much as my mouth. "I just might do that. Thanks for your time."

Chapter 8
Butter, Blondes, and Chocolate Malts

I'd spoken to Dust twice on my way home. The first time I asked him to go over the case files and see if there was any connection between Katie, Beth, and stalker-boy other than graduating together. His second call comes in as I walk down my apartment complex's hallway. The hall, a dull green I've never been fond of, is lit by several sconces evenly spaced on the walls.

"According to our interviews," Dust tells me, "Katie mentioned knowing Stephen from school, but Beth didn't say a word about either of them other than they were classmates. The school records we subpoenaed only told us Beth and Katie were in a theater class together and some sort of planning committee for school dances but there was nothing about Stephen."

"But according to Ms. Sullivan," I add, "They all shared some activity together."

"Tell you what," he says with all the confidence he's known for. "I'll arrange another sit-down with Stephen, and we'll both interview the girls again. Since *you don't seem to be staying out of this...*" he says with much emphasis, "I'll let you pick which you interview. Do you want to take Beth or Katie?"

As I round the corner of the hall, leading to my apartment, I see a blond sixteen year-old girl on my doorstep. Her arm is in the air as if she's about to knock.

"Katie?" I reflexively blurt as if sneezing her name.

"Then Katie it is," Dust replies, unaware I'm actually looking at the girl. "I'll give you a call later."

He hangs up before I can get out, "Yeah... bye..."

Katie, turning my way, exclaims, "Free!"

She runs to me, joyously throwing her arms around my slightly begrudging torso. The girl acts as though we haven't seen each other in years. From my count, it's only been about four hours.

"Katie," I begin, "What... Whatcha doin' here? Is something wrong?"

FREELANCER

Pulling away from me, the girl seems immediately embarrassed. My stand-offish nature is finally getting through and Katie seems to understand she's overstepped her bounds. Taking a step away, her sheepish eyes turn to the floor and she bites her bottom lip as though it's guilty of some crime.

"I'm sorry," Katie practically mumbles under her breath. "I just... I just didn't want to be at home. It's big and empty and.... I don't like being there at night. We had so much fun today... I thought... I thought it would be okay."

Oh, God, she's doing it again – playing my heartstrings like they're a base. This girl tugs any harder and they'll snap. Looking into her timid blue eyes, I can hardly tell her to leave.

"No, no, it's fine," I console with a lie. "I was just surprised. That's all. Why don't you come inside with me?"

Her mood elevates some, but she still seems leery of accepting my explanation. I throw a conciliatory hand on her shoulder just before fishing for the apartment key in my coat pocket. My hand circles round and round before coming up empty. I then search my purse. Lipstick, lip balm, cash, cards, mascara, Mercy – my purse is full of very useful items, just none that work for my current purposes.

My hair flocks forward, pulled by a gust of air from my apartment door suddenly ripping open. Wrist deep in my purse and befuddled look on my face, I feel as though I've been caught with my hand in the cookie jar. My Bad Penny stands before me.

I immediately notice something's amiss.

Her hair is down... and slightly curled. Her glasses, which she wears intermittently, are missing. In their absence, she wears a dark shade of purple over her eyes, a similar shade of lipstick on her lips, and... is that rouge? To cap it all off, she's wearing one of my persona's nicer, yet conservative, shirts.

"Free!" She says with eyes the size of pancakes and a look that says she smells bad cheese. "And... Katie Worthington...? What are you doing here?"

I note she's locked both arms to the doorframe, an obvious sign she is not willing to let us pass. Now I have to know what's going on. Peeking over her shoulder, I can see clearly over the kitchen counter and into our living room beyond. There, on the couch, is a very nice looking young man − someone I've not met before. A littering of textbooks have overtaken our coffee table, while he diligently makes notes in a tablet computer.

My, God... Bad Penny is on a study date.

"Sorry, sorry," I apologize loud and immediately so the young suitor can hear. "I forgot my key."

Turning her stinky eyes from me to Katie, I can see she's even more surprised at her appearance than I.

Through clenched teeth and under her hushed breath Penny asks, "And why is Katie Worthington here?"

Katie, not one to sit out of a conversation, asks loudly, "You know me? Have we met? I'm not very good with people sometimes."

Penny, turning a fiery, sarcastic glare the girl's way, replies quietly, "No, but I've read all your sordid e-mails about some boy named Robert McKenzie, so I feel like I know you inside and out... not unlike Bobby and the back seat of his classic Camaro."

Katie's awkward, friendly demeanor, having been excited to meet Penny, shrivels into utter mortification. I forgot about that. Penny tends to research our clients thoroughly. My girl's not one for personal boundaries. If I remember right, Robert was the guy Katie was rather fond of in high school. I can't quite remember what "base" she let him get to. It might have been a ground rule double. Saving us all from further embarrassment, I launch into some unrehearsed lies peppered with truth.

"I forgot my key and... and just stopped by here to pick it up before Katie and I..." I grab Katie and pull her to my shoulder as if she's now my best friend. The young man finally glances back at us with a curious stare. Huh... he has the prettiest eyes. I can see why Penny likes him... And I completely lost my train of thought.

"Katie and you were...?" Penny leads.

Snapping out of her boy-toy's pretty eyes, I finish, "We were headed out to grab some malts, maybe hit a movie. I just needed to see if my key was here first."

82

"We're going to the movies?" Katie asks, oblivious to any part of the salvage operation I'm spearheading. "Cool, there's this new one I really want to see about aliens or something and these gold –."

"That's nice," I say, wrapping my hand around her mouth. "So is my key here or... maybe the spare?"

Penny quickly fishes an apartment key out of her pocket and says through a fake smile, "Take mine. I'll dig up the spare later."

"Thanks!" I overact to the point of nearly mimicking Katie's bouncy demeanor. Noting the young man has turned back to his homework, I mouth, "I'm sorry."

Katie, still gagged by my hand, flicks her pretty eyes between us as if watching a tennis match. Her mind, which seems only capable of shallow thinking in social settings, has yet to grasp the situation. On the bright side, the girl's so lost she hasn't tried to wiggle out from behind my hand.

Muttering so her young suitor can't hear, Penny jibes, "I don't care where you go, just leave." Glancing back to her date to ensure he's not within earshot, a sweetly sinister grin curls on her purple shaded lips. Giving me a once over, she adds, "And if at all possible, try not to show anyone your underwear."

She is never going to let that go... until I get the best of her that is. Raising a sarcastically menacing eyebrow, I overdramatically look to the young man on the couch, and then back to her.

Devilishly, I reply, "You either."

Point. Set. Match. Penny – the girl who likes to have the last word in everything – is utterly speechless. Without so much as another syllable, the door slowly and quietly shuts in my face, as if delicately putting a lid on this whole awkward situation. I finally remove my hand from Katie's mouth and wipe her combo of saliva and lipstick on my skirt.

"Oh..." Katie says, finally getting what just transpired. "She wanted to be alone with that guy."

And here I was wondering how she skipped two grades. We round the corner and backtrack our way towards the elevator.

"So, can we really get malts and see a movie?" Katie asks with pessimistic enthusiasm. This idea has obviously excited her, but she's tempering her fervor, afraid I'll shoot her down.

Just as I open my mouth to answer, I hear, "What movie are you going to see?"

Looking from Katie to the person stepping off the elevator, I see my shaggy-haired Grant slumbering our way. Oh, just what Penny needs – her little brother barging in. His backpack is slung over one shoulder and his duffle bag over the other. These two pieces of mismatched totes are his preferred choice in luggage when he spends the night. As he reaches us, I don't break stride and snatch his arm as if hooking a trout (not that I've ever fished a day in my life). Pulling him into step with us, the boy is rightly confused.

"It looks like we're all going to the movies!" I say with as much forced joy as I can manage.

Grant, stumbling alongside, replies, "Yeah, that's great, but I need to put my stuff up. I can't bring it into a movie theater and you don't have a car."

"I drove!" Katie exclaims.

"See," I say through my teeth with suppressed terror. "Katie's driving... yay...." Then, as I look upon the sixteen year-old girl and my fifteen year-old Grant, the proverbial light bulb over my head practically explodes with too much juice. "By the way, Grant, have you met the very pretty Katie who is about your age?"

He does not take the hint at all.

"Hey, Katie," he introduces in his clueless way before turning back to me. "I still think I should put my stuff up."

Stopping us in our tracks, I stomp a scolding foot.

"Grant Andrew Blaine!" I chastise. "Two pretty girls just asked you out to dinner and a movie. Do you say *no* to them?"

Grant, in his loveable goofiness, loses all color in his face.

Sheepishly, he replies, "Uh... no...?"

"Damn right," I say.

Noting how I wrap my arm around Grant's, Katie decides to mimic my behavior and merrily locks her arm around his free appendage. We whisk him into the elevator – pretty girl on each arm – headed to wherever the hell isn't here.

"Um," he begins delicately just before the doors close. "I'm afraid to even ask, but can I help pick what movie we go to? There's this really cool movie with gold aliens in it or whatever that I've been wanting to see."

"Me too!" Katie replies in a squeal about as pleasant as a dog whistle in a canine ear.

84

FREELANCER

As the doors slowly close, I look to the overly enthusiastic duo I'm about to spend the night with and realize, while the elevator may stop at the ground level, my night is on a straight descent into my personal hell.

* * *

Twenty bucks says Grant is going to barf.

During the movie, which wasn't that bad by the way – I should give the Junior Freelancers more credit – anyway, during the movie, Grant had a large drink (refilled twice), popcorn (buttered to near-intolerable levels), candy, and cheese-drenched nachos. Now, Grant's built a little bigger than some – in fact, he might be short but he's broad enough that he could rival a linebacker if he ever chose to get in shape - but he's still not someone I thought could stuff that much food down his gullet. It wasn't until we got to the second part of the movie, when the gold people showed up, that I realized my little Grant has an affliction I'd never noticed.

He's a nervous eater.

I'd sat him smack between me, in my short skirt, and Katie, in her short shorts, and we were both eating out of the popcorn in his lap. At one point, when Katie was indelicately scraping the bottom of the popcorn bucket, I caught the expression on Grant's face. He was like some overfilled balloon, at once unwilling to let any air escape, and yet trying not to explode from the overabundance. Once she began licking her buttery fingers clean, in an image no-less provocative than an old hair metal video, the clearly befuddled boy bounded out of his seat – mid-action scene – and headed back to the concession stand.

This was not his finest decision.

While I took a pass on the nacho treats he returned with, Katie was all about the cheesy goodness. Like the popcorn before, Grant had at first set the tortilla delicacy on his lap. And when sitting down with his new snack, he truly believed they were his property and his alone. But before he could scoop up even one nacho, Katie reached over, plucked one out, and lathered it in cheese. His loveably conflicted face was priceless. After all, a pretty girl wanting to share food with him – awesome. However, a pretty girl sharing food with him – terrifying. Teenage boys aren't that complicated.

85

Worse yet for Grant's straining hormones, Katie eats like a lady of the night auditioning for a close-up. She scooped the cheese, so much so it literally dripped from the chip, and instead of letting the yellow sauce dribble back into the container, she held her mouth just below it, allowing the melted goo to drip onto her tongue. I can practically hear power cords echo from Grant's brain as he watches her in slow motion. Absolutely captivated by her devouring ways, Katie essentially swallowed my poor, pubescent Grant whole with that gulp. And I'm fairly convinced Katie has no idea how suggestive a fifteen year-old boy can find the simple act of eating a nacho. In fact, most fifteen year-old boys I've met tend to find anything – including the wind – suggestive, so I can't berate her too much.

As soon as Katie was finished with her first chip, and I saw my young Grant was frozen in hormone induced awe, I picked up the container and set it on the armrest between the teenaged duo, removing some of the awkward angst building in him. He looked at me with such confusion in his eyes. He was like some sad puppy who'd been offered a milk bone but it was behind a glass door. Sadly, Katie is completely unaware of what she's doing to him.

At present, the movie's been over for a good forty-five minutes, and we are finishing up our "healthy" dinners and having desserts. My meal consisted of a hot dog and was followed with half a chocolate malt, which I'm still working on. Katie (how that girl also packs it in I'll never know) had a hot dog, cheeseburger, some of Grant's fries, and is working on a strawberry shake. And Grant... he's in the bathroom. By the greenish hue his face took, I don't expect to see him for awhile.

The booth we're occupying at the moment is in one of those old retro cafés built to look like something out of World War II. Rick's, as it is simply called, is one of my favorite places to eat and right around the corner from our apartment. The counter is stocked with real malt and milk shake machines where you can watch the servers make your favorite treats from scratch. The floor is a tacky checkerboard vinyl and the walls carry memorabilia from classic films and music. Even the servers wear authentic pink outfits with aprons and little hats. Capping off the illusion is a "candy girl" standing in for the cigarette girl of old, offering treats likely just as unhealthy.

Alone with Katie for the first time since leaving the apartment, I know I can't waste the opportunity. The blonde plays with her shake, sloshing the icy goo up and down before taking a sip. She stares out the window, watching each lonely pair of headlights tarry past in the lagging night. She's been awfully quiet since Grant took his leave, making me think she knows what's coming.

"Kate, sweetie," I start carefully, "I need to ask you a couple of questions about Stephen... and some of your other friends."

She doesn't look at me and instead lowers her eyes to the shake in front of her. Her tiny hands continue to heedlessly slosh the pink liquid inside.

"I kind of figured," she hesitantly replies, her eyes remaining on the frothy treat.

Continuing, I ask, "Were you and Beth in some sort of group with Stephen? Is that how all three of you know each other?"

In a firecracker's vicious pop she retorts, "Stephen and I were friends!" I let the stench of her unnecessary outburst leave the air and allow her to continue when she's ready. "But..." she says somewhat apologetically, "We were in a thing together too..."

Her genius definitely does not lie in her descriptive ways or forthright nature.

"What thing, Katie?"

Her chin lowers to the table so she can study the strawberry liquid of which she is so fond. The girl's pretty eyes focus on the drink, like she finds more peace sharing her secrets with the shake than me – as if whatever personal information she shares with it will only be sucked right back into her.

"You talked to Ms. Sullivan, didn't you?" she asks, deflated by the question she must answer.

"Yes," I truthfully reply, "But she couldn't tell me what the group was for. I have to ask you that." With all the sincerity in my heart, I continue, "Kate, you have to tell me what this group was. It could be important in finding whoever is helping Stephen and why they are targeting certain girls."

Katie's face slumps to the side, pressing her cheek firmly against the table as if it's become her pillow. She stares off into the space between her dessert and her apprehension.

As if outside herself, she replies, "It was a group about our parents."

"Your parents?" I reply with little clue to what she means.

Letting out a small breath, she says, "Yeah, Ms. Sullivan called it our *bonding group* or something stupid. We basically met to discuss our parents and... and how they weren't always around... or didn't treat us right."

Oh, no. These poor kids. I was hoping it was some sort of club to get the misfits and popular kids socializing or something else just as vanilla. But that's not it at all. Ms. Sullivan may have called it something else, but at the least, this sounds like a self-help group, and at the most, group therapy. The kids likely never knew.

"Katie," I say, treading ever so cautious, "When you say your parents didn't treat you right, do you mean... they hurt you?"

Her head leaps from the table like an asp angered to strike.

"My dad's never hurt me!" she chastises, creating somewhat of a scene. A few people at the counter turn around to view the commotion and our waitress turns an appraising eye our way as she fills a customer's coffee.

I do my best not to shrink into the vinyl of my seat cushion. I need to work on my tact because I did not mean to accuse her father of such a damning crime... well, not exactly. From the moment I first stepped into the Worthington home, I had already assessed what Mr. Worthington's offense was, and it wasn't some sort of physical abuse. His was a crime of negligence. Even my untrained eye can see this is a girl screaming out for her father's attention.

"Sweetie, no!" I defend. "I... I don't just mean you. What about the other people in the group? Were any of them hurt or neglected?"

Her venomous fangs retract, and her head lowers back to the table.

"Oh," she replies guiltily. The girl is afraid to answer, as if she's concerned she might betray her friends.

"Katie," I say, placing my hand on hers, "I really need to know because this could help people. You might save someone's life."

The weight of my words hang heavier than her misgivings.

"No one ever really said out loud their parents hurt them..." she replies wearily. "But you could tell, you know? The ones who were getting it the worst, they were the ones that always pulled away most."

And there's that brilliance that jumped her ahead two grades.

"We're all rich. You know that, right?" she continues without arrogance. "And I think having that much money makes parents act certain ways... not like... I mean... a lot of their time is taken up by making money. And sometimes... sometimes I think the other parents took out their stress on the kids in the group. Or..." She trails off. Her eyes say Katie has once again left this plain, and her ethereal self is watching her say these words from somewhere above. "...Or, they were like my dad, and weren't ever around when you needed them."

This is a lot to process – even for me – but I need her to continue.

"How many students were in this group?" I query.

Katie, reflecting a moment, says, "Dunno. Ten or twelve."

"So how are Stephen's parents?" I ask. "Are they... mean to him?"

Katie, her blank stare unfocused on the drink before her, factually states, "They're dead."

"Whoa!" I exclaim. "Then, why was he in the group?"

"They just died this summer," Katie continues with a slight shrug. "He wouldn't talk to me at the funeral. Wouldn't even look at me. You think he killed them?"

Well, I do now!

"No, not necessarily," I lie through my teeth. "But it is a possibility I'll need to look into."

I'm betting Dust already knew about Stephen's parents and neglected to tell me. After all, I was off the case. But he may be unaware of the abuse Stephen faced at home. I'll need to call him as soon as we leave.

"What about Beth?" I press. "Did she have problems at home?"

The girl sits back up and her incorporeal stare returns to the land of the living. Her saddened shoulders slouch, while her eyes look to the table in anger.

"Her parents weren't any better than Stephen's," she replies. "At least, that's what I saw. Only happened a couple of times in front of me. Beth wasn't as open about it as Stephen. I couldn't say how often her dad..."

She's too shaken to finish the disgusting truth. These poor kids. The more I Freelance, the more I'm graced with the world's ugliest side.

"I heard you and Beth were pretty good friends for a while," I advise, changing the subject slightly.

"Yeah," she says with a crestfallen heart.

I hate to make a traumatized girl relive some high school drama, but I have to ask, "What happened between you two?"

Shrugging, Katie replies, "She just... things never got better for Beth with her parents... and she didn't like that my dad... that my dad and me..."

I hadn't picked up on it until now, but when Katie talks about her father, she doesn't hold any malice in her words.

"You and your dad started working things out," I finish for her.

Katie nods slightly and says with a sad grin, "When I finally confronted him about always ignoring me – like Ms. Sullivan told me to – stuff changed. We started taking trips together and making plans. It got a little bit better for me."

"But not for Beth," I add with my own drooping shoulders.

"No," Katie replies with a heavy heart. "Not for Beth."

Chapter 9
Is this Lord Childabuser's Estate?

I know it's not proper to speak ill of the dead, but I'm not certain the world's worse off without Beth's abusively theological father. Walking to the front door of their not-so-humble abode, I'm immediately greeted by a man wearing a black suit and tie. The meat per square inch on this guy tells me he is not the butler. His blank, yet suspicious glare and the bulge in his coat – caused by the gun beneath – confirms the family, after recent events, obviously hired security. And honestly, I can't blame them.

Going on eleven o'clock at night, I was smart enough to call before just showing up at the Loughton's home. Beth, while estranged from her parents, had returned there after her father's murder. Although there was some trepidation in her voice when we spoke, she agreed to see me. In fact, by the time I hung up, she sounded downright grateful to have a friend at all. I guess her talk with Dust didn't go so well.

The large, vaguely intimidating man shows me through their palatial estate. We traverse their enormous greeting room with hanging chandelier and marble floor, which costs more per slab than most make in a year. He takes me past a small dining room (I'm betting the smaller of two) with a finely carved table and chairs – just enough for six people comfortably. Further, he takes me through the kitchen and family room just beyond. Both rooms, while I'm sure elegant, are dark and gloomy – much like the mood of the house.

Finally, we enter the reading room where Beth is sprawled across a large, fluffy chair. She's in her pajamas and a book rests gently on her lap as if she'd been reading not long ago. The text has been folded over, her finger keeping place, and her eyes have shifted out the long window. A winded branch softly raps the glass, transfixing the girl with nature's common knock.

"Beth?" I gently say, attempting to stir the girl from her vacant state.

Shaking her head, her eyes regain focus and she turns toward her visitor.

91

"Free?" she replies, barely comprehending who I am. "I'm so sorry. I didn't even..."

Her words trail off. In a disheveled state, she endeavors to put the book down and stand at the same time, accomplishing neither with much grace. For a moment, she almost topples over as she attempts to stand but loses balance. She's likely been sitting in this room for hours and her legs are asleep.

As her personal security leaves, feeling fairly secure the girl is in no danger, she wraps me in a warm, friendly hug. I return the gesture in kind. Beth certainly has a way about her. We've only known each other a day, yet I'm almost willing to call her a friend. Some people are simply cut from the same cloth, you know?

"I'm so sorry," I apologize without any forethought. I had not planned to bare my soul to the girl, but I suddenly feel as though I should. "If I'd only been faster..."

Rearing back, the girl, surprisingly dry-eyed, says, "No, Free... It's not your fault. You saved me. You saved *me*. If you hadn't shown up..."

She trails off and instead reaffirms the grip of her heartfelt hug. Oddly, I can't picture Beth, the girl who supposedly shrugged off Katie, as someone other than the strong young woman in front of me. Finally, after a few moments of quiet assurance, we relinquish the safety of our embrace and take up seats on a nearby, lavish couch. Beth pulls both of her legs onto the cushions as if we're sitting around a camp fire. She seems so comfortable, yet distressed. I can hardly track her mood. Death will sometimes do this to a person. Your mood changes course as readily as the wind.

"Beth," I begin apprehensively, "I hate to do this, but I need to ask you some more questions."

Letting a cautious breath pass her lips, she replies, "I kind of figured that's why you're here."

Placing a sympathetic hand on her knee, I advise, "Some of this may not be pleasant, but please know I'm not trying to upset you. I'm just trying to find who did this."

The girl pulls back, slightly leery of my touch, and studies me with suspicious eyes.

"Beth," I elaborate, "I know about the group you were in with Stephen and Katie. I know it was about your parents."

Like Katie, I expect Beth to shrink, to become guarded and pull even further away. Instead, she stands her ground like some immovable stone wall and shows just as much emotion.

"Oh," she replies without accusation. "I guess you've been talking to Katie."

An odd, dispassionate reply, but correct. Her lack of any sort of marked emotional response makes me wonder how she really feels.

"How did you…"

"You can't trust her, you know," she cuts off, letting a hint of concern in her voice. "She likes to wear one face, but she's a wholly different person beneath."

Yeah, I know. Little trollop is really a nerd. Got it.

"What do you mean?" I say as though I've not seen Katie's better side.

Beth, gathering her words, advises, "She's not someone who can be trusted."

Okay, is this some high school B.S. I'm getting pulled into because that doesn't help anyone?

"She lies," Beth continues. "And she manipulates. She had Stephen and his friends eating out of her slutty little hands."

Whoa! Red flag!

"So she and Stephen were close?" I ask, neglecting to mention Katie already admitted to being friendly with him.

"Yeah, they were way closer than she ever admitted to anyone," Beth replies with a suggestive eyebrow. "I mean… waaay closer. She used him like she uses everyone around her."

I just spent the whole night with Katie. And, while she might put out a certain image, I can't imagine her fooling around with her stalker. She seems too naïve.

"Okay, Beth, I really need you to elaborate," I say in unbridled surprise. "Do you mean Katie slept with Stephen to get… what?"

"Well," Beth says, genuinely concerned. "I don't know if they slept together, but I know she let him do other stuff. I saw it on a few occasions. But, and I hate ratting her out like this, but the girl has issues. She'd… she'd use Stephen's hormones against him. When she'd start failing a subject, she'd turn to Stephen. And wouldn't you know it, suddenly she's doing better."

I'm still not convinced this isn't some high school drama I'm getting drug through.

"So, he what?" I ask, unsure if this is really relevant. "He cheated for her?"

The girl shakes her head and scoffs. She seems disappointed in her old friend.

93

"How do you think she graduated on time?" Beth asks. "The girl is bright, but two grades ahead was too much for her. She needed Stephen just to keep up. I'm not saying she's in on what happened to my..." She swallows hard, too pained to finish. "I'm just saying I wouldn't be that surprised if she knows more."

Well, Katie isn't always the sharpest pencil, but fooling around with a guy to get what she wants? Hell, she was completely unaware of how Grant was looking at her tonight. At least, I thought she was... Could she be that good? Is she still keeping things from me?

As I try to process the information Beth has entrusted me with, my over-encumbered mind wanders to the items strewn about the room, unintentionally cataloging each and every one: A bookcase filled to the brim with books on theology – "True" histories of the occult, religion's influence on society, and murder mysteries; plants sitting in various corners; pictures of her family turned slightly, as if recently picked up and then replaced; a thirty-two inch HG television mounted above the fireplace; a copy of Fantasy War lying on the floor... does everyone have this game? Posh, elegant, and so normal – you would never guess such an atrocious side lies beneath. And I stare at them all, attempting to hide from the ugly questions my new friend's suggestions pose.

I know Beth has warned me to distrust anything Katie says, but I have to make certain of one fact she gave me, which I believe to be true. Standing from the couch, I casually stroll to the mantel. My fingers run from item to item as if simple tactile contact will reveal some secret. When I reach a photo of Beth and her father – a picture slightly turned to face away from the couch – I lift it from its perch. With every intention in the world, I head back to my seat with the photo in hand. My eyes remain on the picture, but my attention follows Beth. Her father, the alleged child abuser, was a handsome man, looking nothing like the evil I imagine he inflicted. Just as my derriere hits the couch and I'm about to comment on what a stately father she had, Beth springs up as if thrust from the cushion by my impact.

Barely breaking stride, she exits the room, calling out, "I'm going to get something to drink. Want anything?"

Her eyes avoid me as she leaves, as if the photo has poisoned my visage as well as the father depicted there. It tells me all I need to know.

* * *

As the taxi nears my apartment, I receive a text message from Dust. He's already looking into the kids from Ms. Sullivan's therapy group. As our font-induced conversation continues, he sends one message that troubles me so deeply I don't notice the cabbie taking me the long way home. It reads:

FOUND OUT WHAT KNIFE IS MADE OF:
PLEXI

After my conversation with Beth, that's an incredibly hard coincidence to ignore. I'm only uplifted when Dust tells me he'll let me know if he finds anything and:

DON'T LET THE BED BUGS BITE

I probably shouldn't grin like some schoolgirl every time he does that, but I can't help it. His silly little assurances impact me more than I'd ever willingly admit. Maybe I should think about... well, Penny called dibs long ago. I couldn't cross my friend like that.

Speaking of, I find it so incredibly odd Katie and Beth have such differing opinions of each other. Beth is distrustful and somewhat disgusted with Katie. Katie, on the other hand, seems concerned and wounded when it comes to Beth. But, if Beth's right, Katie might just be playing me like she did Stephen. On the other hand, Katie is the one who gave me the names of all the students in the group, and she's the one who told me about Beth's problems at home. But now Dust is telling me the knife that tried to skewer me is made of Plexi – the very thing Katie's dad helped make.

Ugh. My head hurts.

Looking up from my phone, I realize the cabbie is taking me down Sycamore, which means he's headed for the alley behind my apartment building. Lovely. I hate the alley. I could stop him, tell him to turn around and go to the front of the building, but it seems so petty. Besides, we're almost there.

The driver pulls to a stop in the alley, which is essentially an "L" of two different roads. One alley runs the length of the entire block and ends at the entrance to my apartment's garage, sitting just behind my complex. The other alley, which separates my building from the apartments next door, runs the length of our complex and intersects with the street directly in front of the building. Unfortunately, the space between the buildings is too narrow for a car to drive through, so I can't even tell the cabbie to keep going. Why every cab driver in the city seems to think a girl really wants to use the back door in a dark alley, rather than the well-lit front door, I have no idea.

Coming to a stop, I flash my card on the cab's credit reader, type in a decently minimal tip, and step out. The yellowish light glowing above the glass and steel back door is battling with the orange garage light in a competition for which can make the alley seem less natural. The only other item making the area even more alluring is the metallic garbage chute running the length of the building and emptying into the dumpsters beside the back door. Scurrying to the door not unlike rats to the garbage, I take out my electronic key and swipe it across the lock. The device's tiny LED light flashes yellow once, and the door remains firmly locked. Again, I run my key across the pad. This time it flashes red twice then yellow once. Crossing my eyes at the damn thing, like it will somehow know I'm perturbed, I pocket my key. The reader is once again on the fritz, and I can hear my cab already pulling onto the main road at the end of the block. Fantastic.

Tightening my red coat's belt, I slip both hands into my pockets and head for the narrow alley leading to the front doors. My feet move at a casual, yet brisk pace. There's no need to be fretful, but there's no harm in being cautious. Reaching the midpoint of the alley, where the yellow/orange illumination of the backdoor no longer touches, my mind attempts to play tricks on me. A shadow moves with benign intent. The wind tosses a discarded candy wrapper down my path, making it sound as though some demonic apparition is scurrying past me. And the clacking of my heels echo through the small road, making my mind want to believe there are two people in the alley, instead of just one.

FREELANCER

Again my feet tend to hasten, but this time my over-imaginative mind calls to attention it is not, in fact, being paranoid. A pair of steps, just off from my own rhythm, have begun clomping behind me. This does not bode well. I could scream, grab my phone, or start running, but none of these options sound especially appealing when you're supposed to be a professional trouble-deterrent. There's also the possibility it's just another tenant locked out like me, looking for a way inside.

Oh, who am I kidding? With a danger-magnet permanently sewn to my caboose, you and I both know it's not a tenant.

My hand firmly grips Mercy, which had been safely housed in my coat pocket all night. The footsteps pick up pace. And just as they reach an alarming proximity to my turned back, I whirl around, extending Mercy as I do, ready to unleash her bludgeoning might on this ass...

The long cylinder and reflective black shaft of the barrel stare me down like the devil's hollow eyes. A click of the hammer, like the tisking of its disapproving tongue, tells me the weapon is not swayed by my mere metal rod. The assailant, Caucasian with a ratty violet hooded sweatshirt and even rattier denim jacket holds the weapon with both hands, as if it could float away if he didn't. From his demeanor, I can tell the man's probably fired a gun before, but he's not terribly confident handling it. This frightens me more than if he was an expert sharpshooter. A novice will kill you without meaning to, while a master is always in control.

Knowing she's useless to me, I carefully drop Mercy to the ground, ensuring the assailant sees my every move as I do. In an involuntary act of contrition, I raise my arms slightly, signifying my docile intentions. The man, jittery and unshaven, steps closer.

Waving the gun in my face, he mutters, "You shouldn't try to be such a hero."

Actually, not trying. Want to resolve this amicably.

Needless to say, I'm not going to say that. Instead, for once, I keep my mouth shut. You don't feed the crazies. They'll turn it around on you and make you regret every word.

"Quiet... quiet, yeah. That's better," he says taking a step closer, "Now, I need you to..."

JEREMY JAYNES

Out of the darkness a hand wraps around the man's gun. His fingers violently twist so the weapon is no longer pointed my direction and the gun falls into this new shadowy figure's hands. The man attempts to turn around, to confront his attacker, but he's met with a swift punch to his Adam's Apple. As the man stumbles backwards, choking on his own throat, the figure, which I can now see is dressed in a grey suit with his shirt unbuttoned – complementing his heroic physique – takes the pistol in his hand like a club. While my attacker gasps for breath, my "hero" wraps the man across the face with the grip. The hooded assailant crashes to the pavement, bouncing off the concrete like it was made of plastic. Unconscious and with a black eye, he won't be getting up for a while.

Putting the gun in his pocket, I hear in a gentleman's, deep Scottish accent, "Ms. Freeman, I do have to wonder why you put yourself in these situations."

My hero, Mr. Ketchum. I shouldn't be surprised.

"I'm a glutton for punishment," I reply, lowering my arms. "Just glad you were here... though it makes me wonder why you're lurking outside my apartment."

"Ah," he says with a laugh. "I was just stopping by to see how your investigation was going. Heard about last night – wanted to make sure you were okay."

"Well," I scoff, "If this is any indication, I seem to be on the right track if they're trying to kill me outside my apartment."

"This is a suspect, then?" Ketchum asks, removing a small, flat device from his coat.

He kneels to the gunman's side and lifts one of the unconscious man's fingers. Placing the tip on the device, he pushes a button causing the small screen to glow.

"I think so," I say, coming down from my adrenaline high. "I mean, what are the odds this is some... random... mugging...?"

Ketchum turns from his device and looks at me with a raised eyebrow.

Coming to my senses, I say, "Ah, crap, I almost forgot I have my life. This is a random mugging, isn't it?"

Dropping the finger from his pad, which I can only infer is a fingerprint scanner, the dapper Scot shakes his head.

"Sorry, my dear," he adds. "Jacob Smith – armed robbery, assault, breaking and entering, multiple drug possession charges – this sounds like a run-of-the-mill junkie."

Are you freakin' kidding me? I need my danger magnet to actually draw the danger I need. Can it not hold off on dragging me toward the crazies until after I've solved this case?

Ketchum removes wire cuffs from his coat and promptly hogties the unconscious man. I especially enjoy watching how he chooses to subdue the perp before checking the man's breathing and pulse. I feel like that should have occurred in a very different order.

"Crap," I say again. "I'm not getting any sleep tonight."

A perplexed Ketchum, standing from his victim, coyly comments, "Typically a woman isn't upset when I cause that."

His flirtatious stare and smug smile cause me to equally gag and swoon – a gwoon. He's repulsive and charming all at once – egocentric and selfless – a gentleman who gets his hands dirty. I'll never be able to put my finger on him, though I'm starting to want to.

Oh, that was a Bad Penny influenced thought.

"Funny," I say with opposite intent. "I just mean I'll be out here all night giving my statement when the flatfoots show up. As many times as I've been interviewed by cops, you'd think it would only take five minutes."

Laughing, the Scottish gentleman advises, "Nah, you don't need worry 'bout that. I'll take care of our friend here."

I'm hesitant to ask, but I have to. For love of God, the guy swoops in out of nowhere and doesn't have an identity I can discern.

"When you say '*take care of*' does that mean I'll hear about him floating in a river later, or will he disappear into some secret prison you have stashed on the moon?"

Ketchum rubs his weathered hands across his stubble and laughs. He always seems to find me amusing. I still don't know how I should find him.

"Regular jail will suffice for tonight, I think," he tells me. "You can visit him in the morning if you like?"

99

Our eyes lock as we share in a moment's good humor. I swear he's like a Scottish Marine stuffed into a super-spy's casual wear. Hmm, now I have to wonder if there's such a thing as a Scottish Marine. Do the Scots have something like Marines? They have spies and royal guards, but...

"So those were nice moves back there," I compliment. "Learn that before or after you were knighted?"

With a wry smile, Ketchum cordially retrieves Mercy from the ground. Lifting the silver shaft from the pavement, he shakes his head in amusement. Like a gift he is bestowing upon me, he carries it in both hands before presenting the weapon.

"Your sword," he says in a very overdramatic manner, "M'lady."

He goes so far as to bow and throw in a slight curtsey. He might just be messing with me, but still, I kind of find it endearing. And did it just get a little warm out here?

"Now you're just being cheeky," I advise with a smirk and swiping Mercy from his hands.

"Yes, well," he says, "Speaking of your plum cheeks, how goes the investigation?"

Hold on. I think I was just sexually harassed. I'd be ticked if it didn't sound so damn sexy with an accent. God, Penny would kill me for thinking that.

"Unfortunately, for my cheeks," I begin with my own wit, "We aren't finding much. Every turn I take seems to be the wrong one."

"Ah, I see," Ketchum says a little too unsurprised. "That's a common problem in an investigation."

"Tell me about it," I return. "I feel like if I keep heading in this direction, I'll be so far removed from the path, I'll never find my way back."

Nodding and listening intently, Ketchum offers, "Maybe that's the point."

My temperature raises slightly, thinking at first I've been insulted. Does he think I shouldn't be on this case?

"Excuse me?" I say with a hint of attitude.

Undeterred, Ketchum continues, "Not everything in life is supposed to take the most direct path. Sometimes we need to look below a matter, or take the long path, while everyone else takes the short one. You've got your mate, Dust, and his flatfoots gallivanting around chasing leads on the straight and narrow. Maybe that's not for you. Maybe you're the girl who looks under the rug, or sidesteps the common path. Maybe you're the person who's supposed to see things from a different perspective."

The overwhelming hope dripping from his words fills me like the blood in my veins. My resolve, which had waned to all but nothing, was blooming like a Scottish rose. Ketchum, through all his shadow and secrets, gave me something no one had in some time. Confidence.

I could jump his bones right here.

Oh, no. Bad, stray thought, bad! Impulses... unchecked... bad... impulses... and only getting worse. With my cheeks flush and eyes all aflutter, my face is letting slip what my subconscious is screaming. And by the bedeviled smile and glint in Ketchum's eye, I can see he's reading my body language loud and clear.

Embarrassment, thy name is Free.

Time to go. All color leaves my face and I stop breathing. Shifting my naughty, mortified eyes to the pavement, I briskly brush passed the enigmatic Scot, hoping to make it to the alley's edge before he catches me. While my shoulder brushes his, I can smell his cologne and for an instant feel his hot breath as his stubbled face turns my direction. I swallow hard and try to press forward. The next thing I know, I feel his powerful hand clasping my arm, gently asking me to stay in one place. I pause, realizing he's inches from me. The stately Scot is so close in fact, I feel each and every warm breath billow into my ear.

"Before you go," Ketchum tells me. "I just wanted to explain – I wasn't just here to see how the investigation was going. I just wanted... I just needed to make sure you were alright."

Every ounce of my lower being – my brain not functioning at all right now – is telling me to turn and plant one right on his incredibly well defined mug. But I'm stronger than my base instincts, and I still don't know this man... regardless of how good looking, debonair, heroic... I was saying something.... Yes, no matter what, I can't give in.

Turning toward him, my face a lip's distance from his, I say, "Thank you... Mr. Ketchum."

JEREMY JAYNES

Pulling from his gentle grip, I exit the alley and head to my apartment upstairs... my apartment upstairs where I may have to find out if a cold shower will work on me like it does Grant.

Chapter 10
Braiding Each Other's Hair,
Making Accusations

"I would have done it," Penny says matter of fact.

"Pen!" I chastise, "You're not helping."

"Just sayin'," she replies. "For future reference, hot foreign dude saves me like that – I'm throwing him to the ground and going for a ride on the trolley – dirty alley and all."

And people wonder why I call her Bad Penny.

She's only kidding – I think – but she's definitely the type to at least admit considering it. Going on 1:00 a.m., I didn't expect her to be up, let alone the Junior Freelancers to be waiting for me too. Katie and Grant are on the couch playing Fantasy War, while Penny and I are having a team meeting at our usual watering hole – the kitchen bar. The pair is so caught up in their game they probably can't hear us, but Penny and I keep our voices down just in case.

"Speaking of going for a ride," I say with a suggestive eyebrow, "How was your date?"

"Wasn't a date," Penny replies, a little embarrassed to defend. "It was a study date – big difference."

"Not if the end results are the same," I contend with innuendo as subtle as a kitchen fire.

Penny, pondering my astute observation through squinted eyes and a mulled chin, replies, "Fair enough. But, for now, since I have no sordid details to share – though I wish I did – we should stick to the case at hand. Come to think of it though, it would have been nice had my roommate taken out the trash before my non-date almost gagged in the kitchen."

Right...

Shriveling at my error, I reply, "Sorry... Pen, I didn't know..."

Her stern, motherly glare is all I need to feel more foolish.

103

"Apology accepted," she replies. "It gave us an excuse to talk roommates. Now, to the assignment at hand." That's my Penny, right back to work. "What did you get from Beth?"

This is the most troubling part. I was informed upon my entrance Katie would be spending the night in the spare bedroom, while Grant roughed it on the couch. Actually, "informed" is the polite way of saying Katie blurted it in my general direction as I walked in but didn't actually take her eyes from the game. Three hours ago, I'd have been fine with her staying over. After my talk with Beth though, I'm not so sure.

"The big thing is Beth doesn't trust..." I nod in Katie's direction, instead of speaking her name. "Thinks it's possible she knows more than she's telling."

Penny's face turns disgustingly perplexed.

In response to her look, I say, "That about sums up my feelings."

"But... but... the little trollop's adorable," Penny says in bewilderment. "I mean... she's not the greatest conversationalist... but look at her with..." She motions her head toward her brother. "He's never been this comfortable with a girl... let alone a pretty one."

I'm glad I'm not the only one finding this unnerving.

Instead of using the bar top computer, a monitor anyone could just walk up on, Penny pulls out her glass tablet and begins rifling through files. I turn my attention to the dynamic duo killing orcs and slaying evil mages from the confines of our couch.

"Looking over all her files," Penny says quietly from the tablet, "I just don't see any connection between her and Stephen outside of school... except..."

I hate it when she trails off. Worse yet, most of the time when she does, it's usually a bad sign.

"Except, what?" I ask.

"Except for something weird Stephen said in one of his messages to her. It said, *Thank you for this. Cronus Falls will finally take its rightful place,*" Penny replies. "Katie's only response was to delete the message – but then she forgot to empty her trash – and hence I found it. You don't think it was code for Stephen's master plan, do you?"

"Dunno," I return with a suspicious eye toward Katie. "What's Cronus Falls?"

"Not sure what it is," Penny replies, looking into the name, "But I can tell you who it is. Cronus was the father of Zeus, Hades, and Poseidon. Get this, the children overthrew their father and Zeus took his father's throne... sound familiar?"

"Katie's and Beth's group was about families," I say with a revelational chill.

"Yup," Penny replies with the same idea.

"And the one person killed at this point... overthrown... is Beth's father," I continue. "Stephen said he wanted to protect Katie... to set her free."

"One way to do that," Penny adds, "Would be to kill an abusive father."

Thinking about this a second, I realize, "That doesn't mean Katie would know Stephen planned it. In fact, it makes more sense if she didn't."

"Then, why would Beth be so adamant about not trusting her?" Penny counters.

We both ponder the gravity of the clue uncovered. I know I'll have to pass this information along to Dust soon, but I want a few more facts first. Looking to the pair on the couch, I see Grant and Katie pull off some outlandish maneuver in their game. The move involves Grant's knight shooting a stream of flaming magic into Katie's axe, as the flames strike the blade she swings, sending flaming projectiles to every corner of the battlefield and turning every enemy to ash.

"Yes!" Grant cheers.

"Awesome!" Katie returns in kind. "I've never pulled that off before!"

Next to each other on the couch, she rocks her shoulder into Grant's in a gesture of congratulations and sentiment. The two are having such a great time together; I'm struggling with what to do next. While I contemplate how to approach the issue, Katie leans over and says something quietly into Grant's ear. He laughs and nods his head. And suddenly I'm reminded of what Ketchum told me – sometimes I need to look beneath.

"Katie," I call. "If you're going to stay here tonight, I need you to do something for me. Call it earning your keep."

"Anything, Free," she says about to begin another quest with her fifteen year-old knight beside her.

"Good because I need you to put the game down," I say like my mother, "And take the trash out right now."

In unison, I get an "Awww..."

"Now! Katie," I lightly scold.

"Okay..." the deflated girl concedes. "Grant, you're the Champion, so you have to pause the game."

"I'm doing it," he returns with some attitude. "I just wanted to level first."

The two begin bickering about whether Grant should pause before or after he levels up his character. Unwilling to let the young pair sort out their disagreement, I end this quickly.

"Grant, pause the game now or I turn it off," I demand.

In a huff, he complies. The screen freezes and returns to a menu where the bombastic, thundering drums of the Fantasy War theme quietly play in the background.

"Man," Penny says under her breath, "When did you turn into my mother?"

I shoot her a look signifying I have no idea. I felt as if Mom's years of nagging possessed me with some maternal poltergeist. Katie, begrudgingly shuffling into the kitchen, opens the retched smelling garbage can. The poor girl immediately gags.

"Oh, my god!" she criticizes, barely letting her breath escape. "Do you haze all your guests like this?"

Instead of complaining further, she holds her nose and lifts the garbage from its container. Grant follows his partner in crime to the kitchen and takes up a spot beside me at the bar top. Considering we make him take the trash out all the time, his puppy eyes confirm he feels the girl's plight. In this instance, as a gentleman he should offer to take the trash out in her place. Oh, the things we must teach him. However, I'm purposefully neglecting to prompt him on such etiquette right now.

"Where?" is all Katie can get out as she attempts to avoid the toxic odor.

"End of the hall near the elevators," Penny informs her. "Big silver chute in the wall – you can't miss it."

Penny grabs the door for her, while I pour a soda for Grant. Both are calculated ploys to split the pair as we need them. The drink gets Grant to stay at the bar. The door gets the girl out of the apartment. Katie, one arm locked straight in front of her, the other pinching her nose, carries the bag into the hall like some explosive device primed to go off. When she crosses the threshold, Penny shuts the door behind her.

As soon as the door clicks shut, I begin, "Grant, has Katie said anything strange?"

Completely taken off guard, the soda in his throat attempts to empty into his lungs. We don't want to rush, but Katie will be back in about two minutes. There's no time to dally.

He coughs out, "What do you mean?"

Penny, the cross examiner, jumps in with, "Has she mentioned her stalker to you at all?"

Considering the strange questions coming his way, he replies, "Only in like brief passing. I can tell she doesn't want to talk about it."

"What has she said?" I quickly ask, suppressing my suspicion. "Even the smallest thing."

Unsure of our motives, Grant suspiciously replies, "Stuff like she kind of missed him...They used to be friends and it freaks her out. She feels – dunno – almost guilty, maybe? I think he took all her friends away somehow and is making her feel like it's her fault. Then he turned all weird." Grant stews a moment, pondering the wounds, physical and emotional, Katie has suffered at Stephen's hands. "I kind of hate the guy. So, why are you asking me this and not Katie?"

Penny attempts to pacify him with, "When it comes to suspects, you can't always be certain they're telling the truth. So, sometimes it helps to hear what their friends have to say."

"Wait! Suspect?" Grant says with great surprise and a dash of anger. "Are you telling me you think Katie – the girl who was your client a day ago – is a suspect now?"

Moments like these are when I remember Grant isn't just a fifteen year-old boy, he's a young man and Penny's brother to boot. We need to remember that in the future.

"She's not a suspect," I kind of lie. "But she's under suspicion."

"Semantics!" he accuses.

Penny, taking the same tone, says, "Where did you learn that word?"

"Dude, I'm fifteen not eight," he replies like the young man he's becoming. "Though you treat me that way!"

"Grant, sweetie," I try to console. "I'm not trying to treat you..." Actually, we are so I'm dropping that argument. "We're trying to make sure everything is on the up and up with Katie, and we want to make sure she doesn't... use you for anything. Understand?"

"Less and less," Grant replies with all the attitude of his older sister. "Are you saying she's going to use me because she's a girl I like? Or, are you saying I'm too dumb to know when I'm being used by girls?"

107

Wow. Which of those do I answer without crushing him?

Penny tries to reply, "We've heard Katie uses guys to get what she wants. We just want to make sure she's not doing the same with you."

Grant, still defensive but at least considering our stance, replies, "All she's gotten out of me is junk food, and all she's gotten out of you is a place to stay – a place not as nice as her own house. On the other hand, what have you gotten out of her?"

"Excuse me?" I ask, realizing Grant is somehow turning the tables on us.

"What have you gotten out of her?" Grant replies, counting the defense off on his fingers. "Need me to add it up? You got paid. You got clues. And you got a list of suspects – seems to me people should be leery of your motives, not hers."

And like that, I realize I can never treat Grant like a child again. He may be naïve when it comes to women – and what man isn't – but we should never underestimate him. I always like to think it was just Penny and I going through all these crazy adventures, but in reality, Grant was almost always there beside us. He's spent his formative years in this world, and he's picked up a lot more than we ever suspected. Until we actually threatened someone he cared about – a friend – he hadn't had the opportunity to stand up and become the young man he's supposed to be. Good for him.

Bad for the case, of course. But good for him.

Wait... is it bad for the case? He has a couple of good points.

"We're sorry, Grant," I say sincerely, conceding to his argument. "You're right."

As if I've spoken in a foreign tongue, Penny blurts, "We are?"

Grant, just as surprised, replies, "I am?"

"We've been given no good reason to believe Katie is hiding anything," I admit. "She didn't tell us she was friends with Stephen before the stalker showed up, but have we found any reason for her to suspect him? We do this stuff all the time, so a friendship on the rocks is a big motive for us, but if I was a normal sixteen year-old girl, I'd never think anything of it."

Penny, deflating to my level, adds, "That's true."

"But," I add with much emphasis, "Because the question has been posed, Grant, you should answer. And if you do, this will be the last time we ask it. Has she done anything suspicious? Anything we should know about?"

Grant, feeling as though he's been given his due, has returned to a less defensive state. He catalogues the night's conversations, the looks he's stolen, the smiles they've shared. Something startling comes to mind and he winces as if pricked by a memory's sharp point.

With sad, disappointed eyes searching the counter, he says with a heavy heart, "Yeah... yeah... one thing now that I think about it..."

Placing my hand on his, I ask, "What, sweetie? Is it important?"

His head so heavy it seems to almost flop off, "It is to me...," he replies. "I think she only wants to be friends... she's not... into me... Not really important to the case though... but worth noting."

Penny, the awful sister she is, in the silence following his confession lets slip an unintentional snicker. The laugh comes on as quickly as a hiccup and is intrusive all the same. She stifles it quickly, placing her hand over her mouth, but the damage is done. Grant flicks his failed eyes at his sister, signaling his lack of humor on the subject. While I feel his pain, I've got to admit, if that's the worst thing about Katie, then I'm relieved.

"You never know," I advise like his older sister should. "She's had a rough couple days. Maybe she'll come around."

Penny and I trade prideful smirks, similarly proud of our little man. Playing bartender for the heartbroken Romeo across from her, Penny pours him another glass of soda and wipes the counter. We sit there quietly a moment or two, letting the young man drown his sorrows, while we await Katie's return.

Then, we wait a moment or two more.

"It shouldn't take this long to take out the trash," Grant says with nervous curiosity.

Penny and I lock concerned gazes, and I reply, "No, it should not."

"You don't think she heard us?" Penny asks.

Unwilling to find out, I nearly knock my stool over as I move for the door. I rip it open and jog down the hall looking for any sign of our wayward teen. Being the middle of the night, the sconces lining the walls create an unwelcoming chasm of uncertainty. Reaching the trash chute, I find no clue as to Katie's whereabouts, not even the garbage I'd forced her to take. Turning in circles, I see no sign of her – no signs of struggle – no signs of anything. Penny, who followed closely behind, does the same.

"Get on your computer," I order, tempering my panic. "Trace her phone now."

Penny doesn't question my demand or even become glib about me barking orders. She darts back to the apartment, passing her brother as he runs toward me. He dashes by and hits the elevator button. One of the two boxes dings open immediately, as if it had never descended.

Before I can ask the question, Grant says, "I'm going to see if her car is still in the garage. Maybe she's still here."

As the elevator doors close, I slip the thumb-phone out of my shirt pocket and hastily ask it to dial Katie's number. Her phone doesn't need to be active for Penny to run a GPS trace. I'm just hoping Katie answers. I'd rather we find out she ran away with hurt feelings after overhearing our interrogation of Grant, than something more sinister.

Her phone rings and rings, but the only answer I receive is the peppy, sunshine inducing welcome message from her voicemail. I dial again. Each ring only prolongs the agony of uncertainty. Once more I'm greeted with her spunky voice, answering the casual caller. And again I frantically redial, this time punching the trash chute and cursing myself for not being more careful. My self-abusive punch, while breaking the skin on my knuckles, did little more than open the chute a fraction, leaving it unscarred. Leaning my head against the wall, directly over the smelly trash drop, I revel in the rancid odor, feeling as if it mirrors the foul stench of my failure. Closing my eyes and letting out a huff, I note the faintest of sounds echoing from what seems like the metallic ether.

FREELANCER

As Katie's phone goes to voicemail once more, I open my eyes realizing the sound simultaneously stops. Quickly, my phone redials Katie's number. Without movement or breath, I listen. There, echoing in the tenuous distance, the bombastic, unmistakable Fantasy War theme music chimes. The theme, resounding with drums but complimented by an elegant harmony, causes my ear to reflexively turn towards the chute, looking for the source. When Katie's phone goes to voicemail one last time, simultaneously ending the familiar Fantasy War opus, I know exactly where the sound is coming from. Ignoring the elevator, I burst through the stairwell door and fly down all eight flights of stairs, losing my heels on the way, without a concern for my feet.

Flinging the last door open as if I'll take it from its hinges, I dart through the lobby and burst out the back door which had locked me out earlier. Dialing Katie's phone once more, I again hear the thundering chimes of Fantasy War. Looking to the dumpsters, I no longer have any doubt this is where the song resonates. Terrified I'll find her pretty corpse stashed in the refuse, but more terrified she's hurt and in need of help, I jump over the short railing separating the back door from the alley and bolt for the dumpster singing the Fantasy War tune.

I tear into the piles of trash bags, flinging them into the alley behind. One after another, I toss them like the unwanted flakes of society they represent. I'm reaching the bottom and still no sign of my blond client. I grab one last piece of black plastic, pulling it from the sticky confines of the iron container, and below it I see my prize.

Katie's thumb-phone... but it is alone.

The girl – my client and Grant's friend – is nowhere to be found.

111

<u>Chapter 11</u>
Have Knife, Will Travel

Grant had found Katie's car parked in the garage, which makes sense considering we found her keys and purse as soon we returned to the apartment. Such evidence leaves us little in the way of hope. We still don't have any firm suspects to think of and the only motive we've found has to do with Stephen trying to protect Katie from her father... but only Stephen's family and Beth's father were out of the picture.

"Penny," I ask, "Any of the other kids in the therapy group have parents that met grim ends this year?"

My Gal Friday doesn't even have to look it up. I'm guessing she already had the same idea.

"Unfortunately, they're all alive so far," she replies not realizing how that sounds.

I add sarcastically, "I'm sure the parents don't feel that way." Penny's so busy going through items on the bar computer, she doesn't notice the jibe.

"You know," she says, pausing on a file. "I can't help going back to this knife."

She pulls up the three dimensional photographs I took of the white dagger Stephen nearly flayed me with. Flicking on the HoloGraph projector, the blade spins as if some murderous top pivoting on our counter.

"I know," I reply. "It seems so familiar too."

"Hey," Grant says with a skosh more manliness than I'm used to from him. "Can I see that a second?"

Grant, not waiting for his sister to reply, steals the virtual keyboard from Penny by dragging it with one finger to his side of the counter. He flips through the HG pictures of the blade. Once he reaches the photo which seems the clearest, he zooms in and out, squinting as he attempts to study the odd symbols carved into the handle.

"Yeah," I say of the odd carvings. "Dust still hasn't figured those out."

Grant as if chasing an elusive thought, pays me little mind, and adjusts the picture so it becomes a wire frame. His head tilts as if he's almost caught the wilily clue alluding him. Growing more curious by the second, he adjusts the color so the odd glyphs are a vibrant blue and the white lines of the blade's edges disappear completely. Our young, typically slovenly Grant steps back from the counter as if he's accidentally primed a missile for launch.

"Son of a bitch!" Grant exclaims.

Penny, ever the older sister, chides, "Language, damn it."

"No, you don't understand," he says turning towards me. "Remember how I said that knife looked like the Blade of Everending."

Looking at the knife again, all blood drains from my face. Considering my crash course in all things gaming this past couple of days, I know exactly what he's about to say.

"That's because it *is* the Blade of Everending!" Grant all but shouts. "It's an exact freaking replica! I didn't realize it when Penny showed me earlier. They played with the glyph's a little bit – they look a little different from the ones in the game, so I guess it's not exact, but still… it's them. This is a replica from the game. Who in their right mind uses a replica sword to try and kill someone?"

"Thing is," Penny corrects, just as shocked but unable to resist her own nature, "These people aren't in their right minds."

"And I have a dress to prove this replica is as deadly as any real knife," I add.

A dazed Grant drops to the stool and utters, "It's all my fault. If I would have looked at that image yesterday… when Penny showed it to me… Katie would be safe and that guy would still be alive…"

My young Grant, ever the noble soul, is suffering the same crisis I did so long ago when I first realized my attraction to danger. You begin to think if you'd been two seconds faster, caught some clue earlier, put the pieces together sooner – but the thing is, at the end of the day, it's not your fault. It's the crazed lunatic with the knife's fault. At least, that's what I tell myself. Though, some days it's much harder to believe than others.

"You don't know that," I tell him. "We may know what the knife is from, and that's a great lead – don't think otherwise – but we still don't know where it came from or who is behind this."

Grant seems somewhat placated, but he's absolutely heartbroken. Even if Katie isn't the love of his life, they were at least becoming friends – something we encouraged him to find.

113

"I need you to get out," Penny, stealing the virtual keyboard from Grant, says to me matter of fact.

Taken off guard, I reply, "Excuse me?"

"I just sent a text to Dust – let him know everything," she advises. "Flatfoots will be here in a few minutes. If you want to find Katie tonight, and not stand around answering questions for three hours, you need to leave now."

As always, her reasoning is sound. I just don't have anywhere to go. Out of the corner of my eye, I see Grant remove his glass tablet from his backpack. He snatches Katie's keys off the counter and tosses them my way. I catch them mid-air like a pop fly and watch as he heads to the apartment door. He opens it as if inviting me through.

"You're driving," he tells me in voice full of manly resolve.

I'm fairly certain he just grew threw inches and his voice dropped a couple of octaves. I've got to admit, I like the take-charge Grant. He reminds me of me at his age.

"The hell you –," Penny begins to chastise for thinking he'll tag along with me.

"I'll help research on the road," he scolds, cutting her off. "But I am not staying here when I think I can help, and you'll be too busy talking to the cops."

Penny and I are astounded by her little brother's clear head. But in a way, I guess it makes sense. He's grown up with Penny and me constantly throwing ourselves in harm's way. He was bound to pick up the same hard shell and level head in a crisis.

"I'll send my file to you," Penny replies, utterly floored by her brother's manly attitude. "Just... just, be careful. Mom and Dad would kill me if they knew I let you go."

I grab my coat and head towards the door. Grant clears the threshold, and I'm right behind when I hear Penny call for me.

"Free," she says with sisterly concern. I stop, letting Grant exit so I can have one last word with my friend. "Please, bring him back in one piece."

Her long look, probing as deeply as I've ever seen her, tells me just how leery she is.

With a smirk and a heart full of sincerity, I promise, "Always."

* * *

114

We're on our way to the only place I can think to go – Katie's. Driving her beautiful, red two-thousand fourteen Ferrari – one of their best years from what I hear – I feel at home behind such a luxurious automobile. Which, considering how I obtained the car, I also feel a little guilty for enjoying even slightly.

Grant, sitting in the passenger's seat, is flipping through our files, while I fill him in on the details of the case so far. He's kept up at such a startling pace, I can't help feel we should have included him all along. Maybe when our cases concern people around his age, it might be a good idea to involve him. I mean, it's not like Penny and I are that much older, but Grant tends to look at the world with such wide eyes, his peripheral vision catches more than our jaded gaze.

"So, they were all in this counseling group together?" Grant asks.

"Yeah," I reply, breaking for a red light. "The students in the group were having problems with their parents, so they talked about it."

Grant goes quiet and reads through some of Penny's notes. If he doesn't have the gist of the group's abusive nature, he certainly will after reading his sister's thoughts on the subject. As I adjust the side-view mirror, I note a huff of breath from Grant and a flush in his cheeks.

Yeah, he gets it.

"Okay, so let's talk this through," he says like the schoolboy he is. "Katie, Stephen, and Beth were all in this group. And Katie and Beth were friends – And Katie and Stephen were friends – But Beth and Stephen weren't friends, right?"

I have to double check his statement in my head twice before I respond with, "Right, but I don't know if that has anything to do with the case."

"Oh," he says somewhat unsure. "But I kind of do... no offense..."

Honestly, kid, you've made more sense than Penny and I have all day.

"None taken," I reply, pressing the gas as the newly green light appears. "What're you thinking?"

"I'm not sure," he says in his little more sheepish self. "But it can't be a coincidence Beth and Stephen stopped being friends with Katie at the same time. Well, I guess it can be, but I don't think so."

Considering his statement, I add, "Beth stopped being friends with Katie basically because Katie made up with her dad. Katie says he stopped neglecting her, and Beth kind of hated her because... I'm not... I'm not really sure why. I was never good at being a girl."

115

JEREMY JAYNES

Petty fights like those were never my thing. When the world crumbles around you on a daily basis, you can't sweat the small stuff. That's why Penny and I are such good friends. Insignificant stuff like boys and popularity never got in our way.

"It's because she feels betrayed," Grant adds with a hint of teenage experience. "Beth liked Katie because both of them had parents that were crummy, but if Katie and her dad started getting along... then Beth probably felt like Katie was better than her... or Beth believed Katie thought she was better than her."

Somewhere in that word jumble, sense was made. Misery loves company. Teenage girls especially can feel betrayed simply by one of their friends attaining a better life. That would also somewhat explain Beth's attitude.

"Yeah," I say, merging into another lane. "But we still don't know why Stephen stopped being friends with her. All we've got on him is something about Cronus Falls. And we have no idea what that is."

Grant turns a frustrated glare outside, watching the street lights pass while hoping to find our missing clue standing on a street corner with a neon sign lit above. When a glowing piece of evidence does not magically appear, he turns to the tablet in his lap and begins typing.

Believing he's looking up Cronus, I add, "I mean: We know who Cronus is – he's Zeus's dad – his dad he overthrew to take over Olympus or whatever. But we don't know what that has to do with anything – other than being symbolic. Stephen, after all, seemed to hate his parents."

"Uh huh," Grant says with an air of disregard. "Well, Cronus also happens to be one of the bosses – the main bad guys – in Fantasy War. He's the last boss a guild – a team – can fight before they ascend to the next plain."

"The next plain?" I ask.

"Yeah," Grant adds, continuing his search on the pad in his lap. "If the heroes win, you go on to become god-like. You become in the game what's called a Warmaster. The player can then watch over other players in the game – you can guide them on quests, level them up, give them cool weapons... or just be a dick and send waves and waves of enemies after them. It's what everyone in the game hopes to achieve."

"But we still don't know what Cronus Falls is," I point out.

Grant, disappointed, replies, "No, I looked it up. It's not a quest in the game or anything."

116

FREELANCER

Driving for a few more frustratingly confusing minutes, I merge onto the freeway and head to New Beverly where the Worthington estate resides. Grant keeps thumbing through items on his pad, while I keep my eyes on the road and my mind on Katie.

Angry with himself, Grant mutters, "What are we missing?"

I wholly agree with the sentiment. As my brain attempts to recall which exit I need to take, a text appears on the dashboard. I'd plugged my thumbphone into the dash when we got in just in case Penny – or better yet Katie – happened to send something our way. The message simply reads:

COPS STILL HERE. DUST SAYS MR. WORTHINGTON MISSING TOO. TRIED HIS GPS. CAN'T FIND HIM. THIS IS GETTING BIG, FREE. CALL WHEN I CAN.

Unrepentant dread runs from my cheeks to the marrow in my spine. Both the Worthington's missing at the same time, and the only image I can conjure is the horrific scene I witnessed as Beth was held captive while her father was sacrificed in some sickly ceremony.

"Free," Grant says, swallowing the lump in his throat. "I know this is bad to say, but they won't hurt Katie, right? They... they didn't hurt your friend. They killed her dad, but... but she was okay, right?"

With all his manly bravado earlier, Grant is still just Grant and crushing him is a real possibility. I honestly don't know what I can tell him. When I arrived at the scene before, I interrupted their "ritual" or whatever you want to call it. So, for all I know, the next step after killing Beth's father would have been to sacrifice her as well. That could be their definition of setting her "free."

"Let's hope not," I finally reply, attempting to pacify myself as much as Grant. "So, let's focus on finding her and her dad. Let's, uh, let's talk about the knife some more. Have you tried looking up anyone selling them?"

"Yeah," Grant says with a squished brow, "I've tried all the stores and typical online sites, but none of them match the ones that dillhole tried to use on you."

I love it when Grant get's defensive of us. Though, he probably wouldn't appreciate that I picture him as a barking puppy.

117

"Thing is," I tell him. "I'm not sure any of the typical stores would carry it. The blade is made of Plexi, and I don't think they'd have access to that kind of material. That's kind of why I thought Katie might be involved. Her dad has access to the stuff by the truckload."

My befuddled Grant ponders this a moment.

"Refusing to believe she is," he makes clear up front. "Then, who else could get a hold of Plexi?"

"Well," I start, "Anyone working with the stuff – the factory workers, scientists, head honchos at Able Corp. There's a long list."

Grant, undaunted, asks, "But Dust always says the simplest explanation is usually the likeliest."

"And Ketchum told me sometimes we need to take the long way," I contend. "Which, by the way, I think we are taking the long way to Katie's. This is taking forever."

"Sure, but aren't we already taking the long way," Grant argues. "I don't think the two are necessarily separate. Shouldn't you look at the likeliest scenario and the least likely?"

I'm getting sage advice from a fifteen year-old. I'd be upset, but he's so much like me at that age – minus the floppy hair and complete inability to understand the opposite sex – I feel he might be right.

"Well then, the most likely person to get Plexi," I begin, "Besides Katie or her Dad, would be someone else at Able Corp."

The cold chill tingling my spine returns, but this time it's warm. This time it's angry. This time, it means war.

"Grant," I say, realizing he's on to something. "Did Penny give you all the files on the students in Katie's group?"

Scrolling through a few pages, Grant replies, "Yeah, right here."

"Any of their parents work for Able Corp?"

Without question, he runs a search for Able Corps' name. In a matter of moments, it has three hits. Katie is at the top of the list. Second is some kid named Randy, but it seems his father had some peripheral work at Able Corp. The third, however, is William Capps. His father runs one of the labs at Able Corp.

"Now," I tell him, "Any way to see if Willy boy plays Fantasy War? And, if he does or doesn't, any way to tell if he made those daggers? Could he have sold them online somewhere – maybe to other players?"

Grant with a light bulb practically bursting with thought over his head emphatically answers, "Crap!"

Turning to his tablet, he punches something up. He flips pages, runs searches, and stares intently at the glass's display as if it too is bursting with knowledge. I make sure not to interrupt his process and casually exit the freeway in silence. The cold stone of the exit's wall and the blue of the LED light posts illuminate our open path. Even in New L.A., once 2 a.m. rolls around, the roads are a pale reflection of their daytime counterpart. When I reach the edge of the exit, as if he receives a shock of electricity, Grant jolts his slouched shoulders into the fine leather seat behind, indicating he's found whatever it is he's been looking for.

"Go to this address!" he exclaims, as his tablet sends directions to the car's GPS.

Looking at the translucent map appearing in the center of the windshield, the arrow points me in the opposite direction. Without so much as asking the young man where we're going, I pull the emergency brake and yank the wheel. Katie's finely crafted, nearly mint, classic auto turns with the grace and ease of an angel's wing. Of course, it also screams and skids like a banshee blazing through hell. Grant, shoved into the passenger's side door, holds the handle for dear life. Unwilling to wait for the car to stop its sideways motion, as soon as I see the automobile's nose is pointed the opposite direction, I release the brake and slam my foot on the gas, propelling us forward.

Tearing down the avenue in the direction the GPS indicates, I ask, "So, where we going?"

Grant, his herculean strength waning as he grips the door, timidly replies, "To heaven if you keep driving like this…"

"Funny," I reply, ignoring a red light I "accidentally" didn't see.

"William Capps rents a house near here," he says, swallowing his bravado back down. "Also found pictures of him on his social network page holding different swords and axes from Fantasy War. He'd made all of them from scratch."

"Awesome, Grant," I praise. "Simply awesome. This is the best lead we've had… well, in the entire case."

Chapter 12
Thirty Minutes or Less

A few minutes later, Grant and I are traversing the broken concrete path leading to Capps' front door, while Katie's Ferrari is resting comfortably in the middle of his lawn.

What?

Someone was blocking the drive, so I had to park somewhere. Besides, for a rich kid, Capps is living in an awfully dinky house with a tiny, untended yard. The crab grass is at an event horizon with the Bermudagrass, which is, at this point, fighting against fate. And, the house with it's chipped, white on grey panel siding has seen better days. This looks like something a college student would rent, not somewhere a graduate from Moreland would live. The front porch is nothing but a slab of concrete, there's a broken garden gnome lying in the bushes, and one of the shutters dangles by a single nail. No, this is not what I'd picture as a rich kid's dwelling.

As luck would have it, there's a light on inside, and we can hear the TV as we approach. Reaching the faded crimson front door, I press the bell. With the television so loud, I can't tell if the bell actually rings or if the button simply depresses out of habit. And, considering the dilapidated nature of the Capps' abode, I'm going to make an educated guess and say the bell is out of service. Opening the screen door, which consists of a rickety silver frame with no glass or screen to speak of, I rap my knuckles loudly against the door, competing with the television's booming voice.

As we stand there, awaiting any sort of answer, I ask Grant, "Are you sure we have the right –."

I'm cut off by the door whipping open and the smell of stale beer wafting through the absentee screen door. We're greeted by an eighteen year-old young man. His hair is black with curls, shirt just a little too tight for his out of shape physique, skin a light cocoa, and eyes as questioning as a lost dog. In his hand he's holding cash, but he retracts it when he finds a girl in red and her teenage companion standing on his porch.

120

FREELANCER

"Wait, you're not the pizza guy," he says in a sleep deprived state.

"No, no we are not," I confirm, still unsure we have the right place. "Are you William Capps?"

Hesitant of our intentions, he replies, "Yeah..."

"William Capps from Moreland Academy?" I ask, trying to wrap my head around why this rich kid would live in a place like this.

Completely misunderstanding why we're here, he adamantly defends, "If you're just another Moreland d-bag here to give me grief, then you can shove it right up your –."

"Whoa!" I say stopping him. Not like Grant hasn't heard it before – likely from me – but still. "We're not from Moreland, but we are friends of Katie Worthington and Beth Loughton's. I'm looking into some problems they've had."

With some revelation behind his voice, Capps replies, "Oh wow, what they're saying about Stephen is true. Man, that guy was always a little off, but I didn't expect him to try and kill Katie."

Grant, using this as an opening asks, "So you know Katie?"

"Katie Worthington? What guy didn't?" Capps replies. When no small amount of horror creeps into Grant's eyes, outing his attachment to the girl, Capps quickly corrects himself. "No! No! Not like that! I mean, a lot of us wanted to – she's hot as could be – but Katie was like this little walking ball of sunshine by the end of senior year and most of us guys had the biggest crush on her. Though, with her being younger, we all figured it was illegal so we kind of backed off... Wait, why am I telling you this? Are you cops? I know he can't be." He points to Grant, referencing his age.

Removing my very shiny, very cool Freelancer business card from my pocket, I hand it over to William. He looks it over curiously, before turning a questioning eye toward me.

"So you're like private security or something?" he asks. If he really did go to Moreland, he might have had some experience with those types.

121

"Something like that," I reply. I take a nice long look into Capps' living room. The room's not too terribly small, but the white paint is yellowing with age and the base boards are chipped and detaching from the walls, as if attempting a slow escape. A crack runs the length of the ceiling, and a windowsill in front of the large bay window has teeth and claw marks where an animal likely perched. The furniture is old, dirty and reeks of stale smoke and beer, while the coffee and end tables look like something picked out of the trash. Opposite the couch is an enormous HG TV affixed to the wall, indicating Capps felt this item was needed more than decent furniture. Not unusual for a middle class kid, considering I expect Grant to live the same way when he finally ships off to school, but Capps isn't supposed to be middle class. Plus, more importantly, there are a few unusual items I can't help note.

"I'm looking into the people who have attacked Katie and Beth," I tell him. "People who attacked them with replica blades from Fantasy War... Know anybody like that?"

On his walls, proudly displayed for the world to see, are several swords and shields carefully crafted to exactly match the game. In fact, over the television are two white blades, a little bigger than the daggers used by Stephen and his lackeys, finely crafted and crossed like a coat of arms. Mounted just above the blades is a silver chest piece with a silver, fanged mask hanging just above – identical to what Mr. Loughton's killers wore.

"Stephen used the replica I sold him to kill somebody?" Capps chokes out in horror.

In a single statement, Capps answers a couple of my most important questions. He's the person supplying our stalker, and he's very honestly surprised to learn about it – meaning he's not likely one of our suspects.

"So," I begin, "You admit to selling weapons to Stephen?"

Shocked by the accusation, Capps returns, "Weapons? Are you nuts? These are replicas! I don't even sharpen them!"

Grant, joining the conversation, adds, "You make a living selling replicas from Fantasy War?"

"I don't know if I'd call it a living," Capps replies, a little calmer than when I inadvertently accused him of being an accomplice to murder. "It's more like a hobby that I'm using to sustain my lifestyle."

I, in my ever-sarcastic way, take a look at his house and say, "That's some lifestyle you have."

"Well, I'm sorry I don't have everything handed to me like your clients," Capps replies with an unapologetic tone. "But when my parents found out I didn't want to be a chemist like Dad, they cut me off."

Grant, taking a closer look inside, seems to fall in love with a molded glass jar on the beat-up coffee table. The jar is very elegant and carries some sort of lettering etched into the side. He slips his way past Capps, making his way to the jar. Timid at first, once he commits, he snatches it right up and studies the carvings.

"You actually made a Cask of the Immortal?" Grant says with enthusiasm. "This thing is amped to no end."

"Thanks," Capps replies with some pride. "I want to work in special effects – you know – in the movies. I want to make props. I make the replicas because – not only do I love it – but it pays the bills and is a nice calling card for my talents."

"Then the armor on the wall," I say pointing to the fanged mask, "Is all for sale? But it's not for actual use?"

"The armor is fairly real, I guess," Capps corrects. "It's really metal and Plexi so I guess it would kind of work, but the weapons aren't sharp. You'd have to sharpen them yourselves. And I don't sell the stuff in here. It's all for show. But I'm glad to make new versions for anyone."

"Like you did Stephen," I add. "What did you make for him exactly?"

Capps' eyes dart to the corner of his mind as if trying to gather the elusive memory.

"I can't remember exactly," he admits, then pulls out his thumb-phone. "But I have it in my e-mail." The young, curly-locked man flips through his e-mail using the HG keyboard on his phone. "Here it is. His guild bought four Blades of Everending, two mages' Warcloaks – the armor you see on the wall – an Emissary's Robe, a Warrior's cloak, two Swords of the Ender, an Axe of the Deserters, and a Staff of Rolak."

"Wait," I reply, attempting to quell my fears. "Did you say his guild? You mean – Stephen had a team?"

With thinly veiled condescension in his voice, Capps turns to Grant and asks, "She's a noob isn't she?"

Grant, not really defending me all that hard, replies, "Hey, she's trying."

123

"Right, well, his guild... or *team*... was Cronus Falls," Capps says with no idea how important his words are. "It was made up of a few kids from school. They were really funny about who could play with them – were like their own private group, you know? Heard Katie was a member though."

Grant, nervous as ever, chokes his worry down and asks, "What do you mean she '*was*' a member?"

"Oh, my God," Capps replies, "They aren't after her because of the guild are they?"

Losing my head due to a severe lack of time, I order, "Explain!"

Capps is literally taken aback by my outburst and takes a step away from me, as if fearing physical punishment if he doesn't answer. Which, let's be honest, just might happen if my patience wears any less thin.

Capps apprehensively continues, "From what I heard... she was... she was one of the guild's big players. I think part of the reason she became so upbeat at the end of the year was she kind of let her normal side – her geekier side – peek out. Of course, the popular girls hated it and... I'm not sure what happened. But one day, towards the end of the year, suddenly all of Katie's girlfriends stopped talking to her and Stephen and his friends – Cronus Falls – seemed to disown her too. If that had been a few months earlier, when she was just another stuck-up Moreland girl, I wouldn't have felt sorry for her. But she really came around in our last semester."

"Who else was in Cronus Falls?" I ask, trying not to imply this might be the most important thing I've heard in the case. "The names of the other kids from Moreland?"

Capps scratches his shaggy head before answering, "Let me send you the names on your phone... you know, if I could get your number?"

I'd be offended if I had time.

"Tell you what," I offer with flirtation about as sexy and forced as a tank through his front door. "You give me those names and I'll think about it."

Capps purses his lips in the corner of his mouth while he contemplates whether or not I'm serious. Deciding he'll take the chance, he goes to retrieve his tablet from the coffee table near Grant. Using this time to elaborate on some long harboring thoughts, my young companion charges back to me in a very animated manner.

124

"I think I've got it!" he says. "The vials of blood, the pictures, and the chalice!" I shoot him a questioning eyebrow and decline responding to the crazy that seems to be dripping from his lips. "Hear me out. In Fantasy War, the Cask of the Immortal is what is called a Hexarbitor."

"A Hex... arboretum?" I question with no idea what that is.

"A Hexarbitor," Grant pronounces again for the slow girl. "It's a... It's a very special... magical gift," Grant explains. "In the game, when you meet a character who needs your help, and they are someone you think you'll want to have around – someone you might strike up a romance with or even just someone you want to treat like family – you give them the this cask. They are, from your point of view, your Penny or Dust."

"Grant, I'm following but I'm not," I have to tell him. "So, what's Edgar Allan Poe's Cask of Amaretto do?"

"Amontillado," Capps corrects, listening from across the room. "She definitely didn't go to Moreland."

"Let me finish," Grant says, stifling us both. "In the Cask, you put a part of your essence – your soul. And if your Penny is ever attacked, she breaks the Cask and encircles herself with your essence to ward off evil until you can rescue her. And the only way she can be fully rescued – in order to make sure no other evil spirits can ever harm her again – is by spilling the blood of her enemy – literally on and around her."

I'm really trying to understand when I say, "So, she breaks my soul-jar to prevent bad guys from hurting her? And then, I make the bad guy bleed on her so his buddies can never hurt her again?"

"Exactly!" Grant exclaims. "It protects her. But in real life, if you were acting out Penny's rescue using Fantasy War methods, you couldn't fill one of these casks with your soul. So, what's the next closest thing you could use as your essence?"

Capps, as if calling out the answer on some quiz show, yells, "Blood!"

Grant turns him an affirming, yet sarcastic smile, signaling he wasn't talking to him.

"But it is blood?" Capps asks. "Right?"

"Right," Grant replies, turning back to me. "But the human body..." he taps the jar to make it echo. "Human body can't produce this much blood, so just like they substitute the essence..."

"They substitute a vial," I finish. "In their minds, it will protect them."

125

"Right! ... and little wrong," Grant corrects. "They already circled the pictures of these girls, thinking or *pretending* they are safe, and then give them the vial. So, they are kind of doing it backwards. Not sure how it adds up in their heads but I don't speak crazy. Point is, they already think the blood protects these girls. Or, at least, they are pretending it does." Contemplating the absurdity of everything he just explained, he continues, "How delusional are these people again?"

Through derisive, pinched lips, I can only reply, "Well, they sacrificed a guy while dressed like characters from a video game. What do you think?"

* * *

Minus Beth and a few other students, the members of Cronus Falls were all from Ms. Sullivan's counseling group. And right now, everything points to them having twisted the game's fantasy for their own sickly gains. Guess Sullivan won't be using this to promote the safety of group therapy anytime soon.

Penny has already updated Dust and he's dispatched officers to every student's address. If any of them turn up missing, then we have our likeliest suspects. Problem is we just won't know where to find them. Grant and I are on the highway again and headed toward downtown. I don't know why. I've got nowhere else to go and no more clues to follow. Even if we have a list of suspects, it's not like we can find them before the deed is done.

"Alright, I found what those weapons Capps made are for," Grant says, having been researching the replicas. "Those are all the weapons you need to take on Cronus at the end of the game. As we all know, if this was some typical dragon or troll, you could just use a Blade of Everending..."

Penny, on the dashboard cam, shoots up an over-exaggerated eyebrow and sarcastically adds, "Yeah, as we all know..."

Sadly, after a single afternoon playing the game with Katie, I actually did know that.

Undaunted, Grant continues, "But to kill Cronus, you need a combination of some pretty heavy weapons – the weapons they ordered from Capps."

"Okay, then it's safe to assume they're really acting out these final battles," I return.

126

Penny interjects from the monitor, "These kids think of their parents as monsters they've been fighting against their whole lives. It stands to reason. And with all the stuff you've seen and replicas they bought..."

"Right," I reply. "Let's say Beth's dad was just considered a dragon or troll – one they were saving Beth from like the damsels in the game. But Katie's dad – the father of Fantasy War – is considered Cronus. If they are acting out the final sacrifice or battle or whatever it is these diluted nutbags call it, then what do they have to do?"

"And can they even finish properly?" Penny asks, "They are missing a Blade of Everending since Stephen got caught."

"I don't think that matters," Grant advises. "According to what I've read online, you only need one for the killing blow. In the final battle, you carry more than one blade in case one of your party members is killed."

"Or thrown in jail," I add in a humorless jest.

"Then the last man standing," Penny says, "Could still kill Cronus."

"So that implies there are at least four guild members involved," Grant continues. "Considering they bought four blades."

"But we still don't know where they are," I say with a defeated sigh. At this point, I really have no idea what to do.

"Yeah, but," Grant begins, "You're Free. Can't we just drive around and we'll eventually stumble across them? Isn't that what you do?"

Penny, noting the obvious cracks in my foundation, states, "Grant, it really doesn't work like that. We might get cases by wandering into crazy situations, but we don't really solve cases that way. Free's not some metal detector you can switch on and off. So we... we just have to focus on what we have. Can you explain how the fight with Cronus goes in Fantasy War? Is there some special ritual we should know about?"

Disappointed and coming to his wit's end, Grant says, "There's not much to it on the player's part. Right before the final blow, the mage does some chanting and casts a spell, but that means we just have a minute or two before they drop the knife. But the guild fights two mini-bosses – big bad guys that aren't as tough as Cronus – and uses their blood to desecrate his temple before the final battle. Basically, the player calls Cronus to the earthly realm by ticking him off and killing his two right hand people."

I think that would be his right and left hand, but whatever.

Grant continues, "One of the bad guys is his wife, Rhea –."

127

Penny jumps in with, "Which Worthington doesn't have since he's a widower."

"Right," Grant continues, "And the other is his top advisor."

"Which we have no idea who that could be," I say without hope.

Grant, without losing sight of our goals, continues, "So, after the War Mage casts a spell on the dead mini-bosses, Cronus appears. Then, the players hurt Cronus' with the Swords of Ender – white swords made from Elven Ivory like the Blades of Everending."

"Ugh, I'm a computer nerd," Penny starts, "And even I feel like my brother is super geeky right now."

"Don't knock it," I defend meekly, my own failures in the case starting to edge into my throat. "Grant's been more useful than I have at this point."

Grant, giving me this puzzled, disagreeing look says, "You saved Beth. That's far more than I've done. I'm just the guy who happens to play a lot of video games. I don't really have any right to be here. I get that."

Even over the camera, I can feel Penny's eyes on me. But I can't face her. If I do, I'll break down. All my fears are bubbling to the surface and my resolve is being replaced with hopelessness.

"Not true, Grant," I say, my inadequacies getting the better of me. "I'm not what you think. You've understood this case more than I ever have. And because I don't know what I'm doing... because I'm just some girl who decided to play detective... people will be murdered tonight. I don't... I don't..."

...Have any right to be doing this. I'm a fraud. I'm a charlatan. I'm just some dumb girl with a lot of bad luck who decided to stick my nose into other people's business. I'm completely responsible. I'm... I'm...

"You're full of shit," Grant says with more determination then I've had all day, "You know that?"

Penny, ever the friend and older sister, adds, "I'd complain about his language, but he's damn right."

"How many people have you saved in your lifetime?" Grant asks without letting me answer. "And two of those people, by the way, are speaking to you right now."

He's right. That's how I met my Bad Penny and Grant. They were caught in the middle of one of my danger magnet's freakish events. And, like I always try to do, I pulled them out.

"You may think you don't know what you're doing," Grant tells me, "But that's not true. You have more experience with the crazy dangerous stuff than anyone... possibly on Earth. You've lived a cop's life since you were born. So, don't flake-out on us now!"

"Especially when," Penny adds with a bit of a smile, "There's a cute girl involved that my brother likes."

Grant, instead of getting offended, jokingly replies, "Exactly!"

I wish I had recorded this conversation. If anyone ever asks why I keep these two around, this would be exhibit A. Penny is the best at reminding me of who I really am. Sometimes that involves putting me in my place when I'm getting too full of myself. Other times, it involves pulling me up when I lose my way. My sweet Grant is picking up these traits nicely, and I couldn't ask for better friends.

"Okay, I get it. I have to save the girl," I say, wiping a tear from my face. I take a deep breath as if cleansing all the negative energy attempting to overwhelm me. "Then, if we're going to do this, we need to go over the facts again. Pen, what do you have from Dust? Anything new?"

I hit the blinker and head to the freeway exit. The concrete slope guides me toward the neon and LED glow of downtown. For no reason other than it sounds good, I take a left at the first light we come across. Penny flips through her notes and organizes them into something legible.

"Stephen's still not talking," she begins from her notes. "Said he was trying to set Katie free – which, now that we've talked about it, could indicate he's treating her like the damsels in the game. Blade he tried to kill you with was made by Capps – who also made a bunch more for Stephen's friends. Katie used to be in the guild of crazies with Stephen. Cronus Falls is the guild and Cronus was overthrown by his son, Zeus. Guild looks like they are preparing to kill Cronus – Katie's dad – in real life, but we don't know where. Cops searched Stephen's home and broke into the Worthington house just a little while ago but didn't find anything. Flatfoots should be arriving at the guild members' homes as we speak. And... that about covers it."

"Hold on," I say, something coming into focus. "They broke into Katie's house? No one was home?"

Penny flips through her notes to double check before replying, "That's what Dust said. When no one answered, he broke in. Hope he had a warrant." Looking up from her notes, Penny catches the wheels turning behind my eyes. "What are you thinking, Free?"

129

"Candace – Ms. Sheldon," I begin, "She's the Worthington's housekeeper. She lives with them. She's very close to the family..."

Penny, getting my meaning, continues, "She should have been home. And she fits the description of both Worthington's wife and his chief advisor."

Grant, rightfully questioning, asks, "So you think they took her too? But do you think they'd accept a substitute like that?"

"They weren't done when I interrupted them with Beth," I answer. "But, since they had already killed her father, they amended their plans. I don't think minor changes will stop them."

Penny adds, "It's as if they're delusional, but just sane enough to know what they're doing."

"Let's hope the courts feel the same way," I reply. "Grant, where did you say they fight Cronus?" I take the next right I come to, though I have no discernable reason why.

Grant, unsure why I'm asking, replies, "His temple, but Penny said the cops already searched Katie's house."

"Yeah, but," Penny adds, having the same thought as I. "That's not his temple."

Curious as to what his big sister knows that he doesn't, Grant asks, "Then what is?"

With a sense of good fortune, I look down the block. I shouldn't be surprised my magnet drew me here, but I've never thought of it as my ally until today. My finger and sly grin point to Grant's answer. He follows my long, chipped nail into the sky. Just ahead of us he finds the large illuminated sign of Sensation Limited – home to Fantasy War and the office of Mr. Worthington.

Grant, with one part relief and two parts fear, says, "And you said we wouldn't wander right into it."

Chapter 13
Next Floor: Firmware, Spyware, and Masked Killers

"You left my brother in the car, right?" Penny asks in my earpiece.

"Of, course," I reply with Grant standing right next to me in the elevator. "Now, when will Dust be here?"

"He's ten minutes out according to GPS," Penny replies. "But he says he'll be there in five."

The agonizingly protracted elevator ride to Mr. Worthington's office on the top floor rubs my last frayed nerve raw. I had actually intended on leaving Grant behind, but he insisted upon coming along. Tired of arguing, I armed him with a crowbar from Katie's trunk and gave him my spare earpiece – the one that doesn't look like a woman's earring. We trekked to the elevator in the building's garage. The Higgten Tower, home to Sensation Limited and several other companies, has rigorous security – none of which seems to be on duty tonight.

"Know why you're alone?" Penny asks in a downtrodden beat. "Kevin Higgten, owner of Higgten Tower, has a son by the name of Jeffrey – a son who happens to be in Cronus Falls."

"Daddy dearest still alive?" I ask of Mr. Higgten.

"For now," Penny replies. "Imagine he's on the Cronus Falls' kill list somewhere though."

More glib than serious, I reply, "I'm starting to feel like Fantasy War is evil."

"No," Penny corrects. "People are evil. These kids could have been fans of Sherlock Holmes and still would have found a reason to kill their parents. They just would have been wearing a lot of tweed when they did it."

Grant laughs and mutters so his sister won't hear, "Yeah, but they would have been smoking pipes, and second hand smoke kills, you know." Thankfully, the earpiece's mic is off. Otherwise, his sister would have heard even the tiniest whisper.

My knotted stomach unties slightly with the jokes.

131

"Still," I add, "You've got to wonder what pushed these kids to this point. What made them collectively decide to band together and go this far? And how did they even know the other kids would go along when they brought it up? Wonder if their team leader – their Warmonger –"

"Warmaster," Grant corrects for only my ears.

"— wonder if he or she led them down this path."

Grant quietly advises, "The Champion is the team's – the guild's leader. Warmaster is the invisible person pulling the strings. You could at least try to get it right."

"Wonder if the leader subtly approached the other kids," Penny adds, fortunately avoiding the terms *Warmaster* and *Champion*. "Used their common pain to unite them."

Grant, under his breath, replies, "Maybe that's why they kicked Katie out. Whoever their leader is – the Champion in the game – knew she'd never go along with it."

A valid point, though, I don't have time to ponder it as gravity has shifted, indicating our upward momentum has come to an end. With a ding and a woosh, the metallic doors slink into the slots beside. The hallway beyond our large metal box is sparsely illuminated with glowing blue sconces lining the walls. No other light, except for the barely lit fixtures, creeps into our path, creating strange, blue upward "V" formations on the wall across from us. The lower half of the walls and floor are engulfed in soulless black. The sight is so ponderous, I have to wonder: When we step from the safety of our motorized box, will we be sucked into some black vortex below?

"Just so you know," Grant says in a slightly humorous tone, "If I get sacrificed by some dude chanting klaatu barada nikto, make sure to leave out the part where I scream like a little girl."

"Klaatu barada what?" I return, nearly laughing but fear getting the better of me.

Grant grips his metallic rod with white knuckles and inches forward as if he's going to step in front of me – to protect me while we exit. What the boy lacks in bravado, he surely makes up for with intent. Not willing to let Penny's little brother forge into the darkness without his guardian angel, I spread my wings and fly right in front of him as we depart the elevator.

My heeled foot clacks on the dark floor below, echoing to a degree I care not think. My mid-calf boots, while a smaller heel than the shoes I lost on the stairs, probably weren't the most sensible item I chose to throw on today. I'll have to start rethinking my wardrobe options... should I live beyond the next five minutes. To ensure a fighting chance, I slip them off and leave my footwear next to the elevator doors. I'd rather go barefoot than announce my approach.

"Where am I going, Pen?" I ask quiet as a mouse.

Penny had tried to access the building security cameras. They were inconveniently off-line.

"According to the schematic: On the other side of the wall you're facing is the main floor for Sensation. It's where the main programmers are housed. There won't be much to hide behind since it's basically one big open room. Then, across this wide open area, you'll find a staircase leading to Mr. Worthington's office. It overlooks the whole floor."

I'm not overly-joyed by this information. My only solace comes from the dullness of the lights and the noisy hum of an overhead exhaust fan. The device, designed to keep the heat produced by so much computer equipment to a minimum, seems to pull as much sound from the room as it does warm air. Making my way to the edge of the hall, I lean around the corner to spy the main floor. Penny's assessment was correct. There before me is a field of plastic and metal desks, cropped into neat rows for the programmers to till. Like the hall before, a few sconces are affixed to the walls and the two large, concrete pillars standing in the center of the room. The fixtures provide just enough illumination to make out silhouettes but little else. However, the sconces' are of little merit right now. No, the strange blue light emanating from the glass office overlooking the floor – Mr. Worthington's office – is demanding my attention at the moment. Movement from various figures in the room demands my gaze further.

Grant nervously peers over my shoulder, stealing his own look at the main floor. Something catching his eye, he quickly taps my shoulder like he's trying to extinguish a flame. When I give him my semi-annoyed attention, he immediately points to an area across the room and just below the stairs leading to the office. My eyes shift their focus and strain to note whatever it is the young man sees. All I can make out are the silhouettes of a cubicle, a high-backed chair, and a coat hanging nearby.

Then the coat moves.

133

The movement is slight, as if someone shifting his or her weight from one leg to the other, but it is not imagined. That is no coat. It's another of the hooded figures.

"They've got a watchdog," I say in a hushed tone.

I pull back around the corner and grab Grant's collar to ensure he follows.

Grant, eyes as wide as saucers but ready to assist in any way possible, asks, "So what do we do?"

Good question. Multiple scenarios run through my head. We could pull the fire alarm, but that would alert them. I could have Grant create a distraction, while I sneak by. But I would like to avoid putting Penny's little brother directly in harm's way. We could both sneak around, jump the person, but that option also means they could turn around and skewer us at a moment's notice.

"Pen," I say. "We've got someone in our way. When I give you a signal, is there something you can do to distract this person?"

She doesn't come back for a few moments, but I can hear her working away on her computer.

"I think I can cook something up," she replies. "I'll let you know when it's ready... wait. Did you say we?"

Hand in the cookie jar, I meekly defend, "Grade my grammar usage later. I'll tap my earpiece when I'm in position."

Turning to Grant, I hold a single figure over my lips telling him to stay quiet. I then point that finger directly at his feet, indicating he needs to stay put. Gripping Mercy, I slink from the hallway and onto the main floor. My bare feet pat the cool linoleum for a few steps just before landing on a small area rug someone threw under their desk. Since the walls are lined with the faint sconce light, I hunch down and choose to move down a row of darkened cubicles about ten feet from the walls. My eyes strain to keep track of the dark figure lurking below the stairs, but I can see he or she has not moved, or, better yet, hasn't taken notice.

Having passed seven or eight desks, I've got about a dozen to go when the door upstairs opens. I stop dead in my tracks. Another figure, this one wearing a fanged silver mask, has emerged onto the small landing overlooking the room. Slowly, I shrink lower than the desk beside me and collapse onto my belly hoping I haven't been spotted.

"We're almost ready," the male in the fanged mask calls over the whirring fan above. "You'll need to be up here when it begins. I'll give you a call when it's time."

134

FREELANCER

The figure below the stairs doesn't respond, which is fine with me. In my new proned position, I slowly crawl across the floor, hidden behind the desks. The area rugs have become limited and I am now slinking over the cold linoleum floor more often than not. Finding my red leather coat too cumbersome for such movement, I slip it off mid-stroke and continue forward. Time is limited now. I've got to keep going at this modest pace and hope I don't...

My elbow smacks the roller ball on the desk chair directly next to me. The room being so dark, I thought I had cleared it. The small black chair, weighing practically nothing, rolls mere inches on the linoleum, but even that should be enough. The fact it smacks into the desk next to me in a loud clack only makes matters worse.

I know in mere seconds, I have to be as far away from this desk as possible. Suppressing my panic, I look to the row of desks on my right side. The closest faces me and carries a gap about ten inches high between its smooth glossy front and the floor. With few options available, I attempt to squeeze under. My arms go through with no problem and to ensure my cranium's passage I turn my head to the side, brushing my cheek across the floor. The next test is my back. I squeeze my headlights into the floor, mashing them like air trapped in folded sheets. When I sail through, as though my efforts were wasted, I'm more than a little offended. I thought my boobs were bigger. And I'm not even going to address how I feel about the fact while my chest isn't big enough to cause even minor alarm, my ass can barely squeeze under.

Arriving on the other side of the desk, my hand smacks the chair here as well. Thankfully, I kind of expect it this time and grab the chair to prevent any forward motion. As I curl into a ball, carefully tucking my arms and legs under the desk, I hear the approaching footsteps of the Cronus guardian. The figure cautiously approaches my last location with slow, deliberate strides attempting to check each nearby desk's shadowy space beneath. Unable to inspect the darkness with any certainty, the guardian removes a small flashlight and shines it on the desk I had disturbed just moments ago. The cloaked individual, obviously feeling unsatisfied, shines its light to the left of the desk and then the right.

I chance a peek through a small hole in my hideaway's exterior likely used for wiring. The person, wearing deep red and white robes, finds nothing and turns the light towards the next desk in the row. Removing a white dagger from beneath the robes, the guardian kicks the next desk as if expecting someone to leap out. When no one does, the figure wanders off, headed to another row out of my eyesight.

Now I've nowhere to go. Unable to see the robed guardian, any movement on my part is a serious risk. I could chance it, and I may have to, but it's not the optimal plan. Then again, if the guardian makes its way to the elevators, it may discover Grant. Ugh... I hate having limited options. And, in less time than it would take to snap my fingers, the choice is made for me. As if heaven's blinding light bursts through the ceiling to shine only upon me, streams of literal light beam through the holes and cracks of my desk. The guardian's flashlight has turned my way. I grip Mercy with one hand and tap my earpiece with the other. Hopefully, whatever Penny's distraction is, it'll leave me enough time to stun the crazy white-knifed person headed my way.

I hear the shuffling of the robed guardian's feet on the opposite side of the desk. The murderous individual circles like a hawk above prey. But this prey has talons too and hopes to use them. As I await Penny's distraction, my bones chill and my cheeks grow cold. For a moment, I can tell the robed figure is standing very still, frozen beside the desk. Then, as if an apparition disturbed, the light is gone and I can no longer disseminate where my pursuer has fled. Holding my breath, I listen for the smallest of sounds to indicate where the guardian has disappeared to, but the buzzing of the fan above prevents even that.

As suddenly as a clap of thunder but with the surprising festive tones of a mariachi theme, a cell phone rings. On a different occasion the ringtone might be funny, but not when the sound is chiming directly in front of my hiding place. The robed figure's flashlight clicks on and a white dagger plunges toward me. Out of sheer reflex, Mercy flicks upward to deflect the blade. Still curled in my ball and a crazed cloaked figure standing directly before me, I've nowhere to go and the confines of my hiding place convince me I've exhausted my last defense. The figure's shoulder twists as if preparing for the killing blow. Staring at the sharp, merciless blade set to end my life, my mind freezes and I can think of nothing but the terrible sensation I'm surely about to feel when the weapon plunges into my chest.

FREELANCER

Out of nowhere, I hear a dull clang and the figure, as if taking one shot of liquor too many, stumbles to the left, then the right just before dropping to its robed knees and collapsing onto its face only inches from me. The guardian's flashlight rolls into my hiding spot and I quickly snatch it up, pointing it in the direction of my savior. Out of the darkness, like some champion of old wielding his mighty crowbar dubbed Excalibur, steps Grant. He offers his hand in an effort to help me from my would-be deskly coffin. Without any conscious thought to speak of, I take his hand and switch off the light. Call it adrenaline. Call it being overwhelmingly grateful. Call it a bad idea. They all apply. But I can't help it. With no forethought at all, I plant a quick peck on his lips, then take him into the biggest, strongest hug I can conjure.

"What happened?" Penny calls over the earpiece. "Did I hack the right phone? Did we get him?"

Still holding onto Grant for dear life, I reply, "Grant got him. He saved me." I'm still in shock. Normally, I wouldn't go all wimpy, but that was as helpless as I've felt in a long time.

"Grant?" Penny exclaims. "You told me he stayed in the car!"

"Hey," Grant says, switching on his earpiece's mic. "Saved Free from a big, menacing killer. Think I deserve some credit."

Releasing my bear-like grip from the boy, I regain my senses. Stooping to the unconscious body on the floor, I pull back the hood in an attempt to identify our attacker. Oh, Grant may not feel quite so manly here in a second.

"Actually, Grant," I can't help correct, "Not so much *big* and *menacing* as *medium* and *brunette*."

Grant takes a look at his fallen victim. Our crazed Cronus guardian is a girl that's a tad bigger built than I, but smaller than Grant. She's not exactly the poster of ferocity he had in mind.

"Oh, dude," Grant says woefully. "I just clocked a girl? That's... awful. I'm going straight to hell."

"Don't feel too bad, baby brother," Penny replies. "She was going to kill Free. You did the right thing."

"Yeah," I add, "You officially have permission to hurt any girl – physically or emotionally – who is trying to kill or maim me."

"Or me!" Penny interjects. "Though... I would prefer you were *not* in a position to do so." That comment was aimed more towards me. I can take the hint.

"So," Grant begins, "Now, what's the plan?"

Looking at the robed body on the floor, I have the perfect idea.

137

"Grant," I say landing a friendly hand on his shoulder, "Today is your lucky day. You get to strip a girl's clothes off and tie her up."

Sadly, it will take him three minutes to figure out this is not as much fun as it sounds. Removing the girl's robes, I slip them on only to realize she is much shorter than I. In fact, Grant would probably be closer to the right size. I pick up the white dagger and slip it into a sheath hidden below the first layer of cloth just before tucking the flashlight into another pocket. I'd only just pulled the robe's hood over my head when Mr. Worthington's office door opens upstairs. I immediately shoo Grant away. My young champion darts to the next row of desks, as if he'll make a mad dash back to the elevator hallway. He makes it about half way down the row before he realizes he'll never make it in time and slides beneath the nearest desk, banging his head along the way. The fanged figure, a "War Mage" or something like that, walks to the railing on the staircase. Realizing I'm taller than his accomplice, I bend my knees so the robe scrapes the floor, and I pull my hood lower. The room's darkness should obscure my face, but there's no need to take the chance.

"Guardian Sol," the fanged man calls. "We are ready. You should join us in --."

His voice trails off, and I know exactly why. Although half a row away, I can hear the desk chair roll from Grant's hiding spot, smack into the desk behind, and then topple to the floor. My accident-proned champion just gave himself away. I squint my eyes in horrified disbelief – yet chastise myself a little for being at all surprised. So, with little recourse, I can only do what comes natural.

Improvise.

Quickly and frantically, I flip on the flashlight and turn it Grant's way as if I too noticed the sound. I take a step toward the overturned chair, but stop as if cautious of what I'll find. In my peripheral vision, I can already see the War Mage has taken a few curious steps down the staircase. Purposely, I pause and turn the killer's way. I wave my flashlight frantically, asking him without words to join me, before turning back to the desk. The fanged man hastily makes his way down the stairs and moves to my position. His pace slows as he nears me, and I can only pray he's doing so out of caution for whatever is under the desk, and not because he's noticed I'm not his murderous friend.

Luck be a lady named Free tonight. The War Mage passes me by and removes a long white sword from his robes. He holds the weapon just like a character from the game – proud and noble as if ready to slay a beast. Mimicking the unbalanced young man's actions, I too reach inside my robe for a weapon and move behind him. With every inch he closes on Grant's hiding spot, the War Mage raises his sword slightly higher as if readying himself to bring it down upon the intruder's head. And with every inch, I step ever-more slightly behind his back. When he's finally within striking distance, I inform the ill-fated Cronus Falls member of the weapon I'm holding. Actually, I don't so much as tell him. I let Mercy and her five hundred thousand volts do the talking. The War Mage's entire nervous system goes into shock and every muscle in his body convulses as he launches over the desk and smacks into the linoleum floor on the opposite side. His big, white sword clangs at my feet where he once stood.

"Holy crap, Free," Grant says as he rolls out from under the desk. He stands and brushes off his baggy clothes. "I thought you were going to let that guy sacrifice me."

"Not hardly," I say with an assuring pat on the shoulder. Looking to the office upstairs, my plan just got a little more complicated, and Grant may or may not like it. "Remember how you got to take a girls' clothes off earlier?"

"Yeah," Grant returns extremely suspicious of what I'll say next.

"Well," I begin, looking the War Mage's way. "Now you get to take off a boy's clothes. On the plus side, I'm sure you've always wanted one of these costumes."

Surprisingly, Grant doesn't complain. I think the intensity of the situation finally landed its blow. Going by the War Mage's words, we have precious few moments before Katie and her father might be killed. Hastily, I slip off the robes too short for me, and don the War Mage's cloak and mask which fit more accurately. Grant, eager to help but terrified into a muted state, wraps himself in the Guardian's robes and slips the white dagger in its sheath. Picking the sword up from the ground, I return it to the long leather covering on my back. Mercy, on the other hand, I collapse into her smallest form. I slip her up the long, violet sleeve of my costume – hidden and being held there by the palm of my hand.

Turning to Grant, I say, "Just follow my lead and try to get as close to the hostages as possible."

Penny cracks in, "Dust is almost there. Think you can stall them?"

139

My unsure face, thankfully hidden behind the fanged mask, replies, "We'll do what we can."

Trudging up the stairs, I attempt to keep my calm. I'd like nothing more than to sprint up them, rip the door open, and show these nutjobs a whole lot of Mercy. But for all I know, I could get someone killed. So I carefully, casually make my way to the office with Grant in tow. As we approach the door, the strange blue glow intensifies and bathes the entire landing. The ominous illumination seems to overpower any other colors in the area and wash them out in vibrant sky blue. Oddly, the glow seems to stop as if hitting a wall, and ends at the landing's edge without so much as a blue streak touching the open area below.

I can see silhouettes in the office, but the light reflecting off the glass is too intense to make anything out for certain. Opening the door, the polite side of me says I should hold it for Grant, but the protective side marches through first. Not having a clue how the person I'm impersonating normally acts, I put on my best monk's walk, ambling slowly as if observing this sacred event. Grant, his hood pulled down to mask his face, can see very little but my feet, and does his best to keep stride.

The center of the office, which happens to be as large as Penny and I's living room and kitchen combined, has been cleared of all furniture with the desks and chairs shoved against the far wall. The first figure I note is a large dark robed Warrior directly across the room. How do I know he's a Warrior? He's the one wearing similar robes, but wielding an axe the size of Grant. Standing next to him is a blond man, roughly forty years old, with the same soft features as his daughter – Mr. Worthington. Gagged and his hands bound, the tip of the axe rests just below his jaw, holding him in place. Next to him is another War Mage with a silver fanged mask like the one I stole from his unconscious partner. The delusional wizard presides over a most disturbing, yet thankful scene. Ms. Sheldon is bound by her wrists and ankles, while a white piece of cloth gags her mouth. She lies on the floor, encircled by a strange symbol. Her eyes widen in terror and plead through a series of muffled cries for someone to save her. A white dagger in the War Mage's hand, I know what awful event comes next. But all I can think is, "Thank God she's still alive."

Most perplexing though is this hovering blue orb. The seemingly self-propelled light bounces near the ceiling directly above Ms. Sheldon. The light, while intense, seems to come to a point in the room, then tapers off to nothing, leaving the corners of Mr. Worthington's office as black as night's peak. I honestly cannot make out what could be causing its glow. More troubling, Katie is nowhere to be found and I can only hope she's captive in one of the darkened corners where I cannot see her. I also have to hope there's not some hidden Cronus Falls member lurking in the shadows because what I plan to do next could get us all killed.

Noting the symbol encircling Ms. Sheldon on the floor, I approach it and circle its right, toward the Warrior. Grant, trying his best to make this look convincingly ritualistic, circles the opposite way toward the War Mage. Recognizing him as the greatest threat in the room, I stroll closer to the axe wielding Warrior. I'm not fond of Grant approaching the War Mage, but at least the mage has to levy his weapon in offense. The Warrior only needs to flinch.

"Locutious," The fanged Mage calls in a raspy, low tone. The person seems to be lowering their voice by several unnatural octaves in an effort to conceal their identity. I can't even tell if this is a boy or a girl.

Wait? *Locutious*? Isn't that a type of lipstick?

"My brother," the young crazy person continues. "Would you please hold your place and begin the ceremony."

Crap. I'm still a good five feet from the Warrior. If I whip out Mercy now, I'll probably get Mr. Worthington killed. Questioning what I'm supposed to do, I glance at Grant, hoping he might throw me some hint. While his face is still completely masked by his robe, and my own is hidden behind this fanged mask, I could swear he shrugs in response. Yeah, I don't think he knows the ritual either. The butterflies in my stomach are turning into pterodactyls trying to claw their way out. I'm sweating – nervous – ready to faint!

Hmm... there's a thought...

Oh, danger magnet, don't fail me now. In a courtly move worthy of a King Arthur, I ceremoniously unsheathe the white sword on my back. Bringing it down ever so slowly, I begin to mumble so low the Warrior and mage cannot hear me.

"Klaatu... barada... nikto..." I mutter as if performing some ceremony but inadvertently speaking too low for the congregation.

141

As the sword stands straight out from my arm, I let it waiver slightly, then more and more, as if my strength is waning. Finally, my arm wilts to the ground and the sword falls from my grasp in a sharp clang. One of my hands goes to my side as if in pain, while the other hand claps my forehead as if my mind is leaving me. I stagger and sway.

The Warrior, surprised at my sudden illness, calls, "Locutious? Kevin? You alright?"

Dude named himself after lip balm and dressed like a wizard to kill people. Kevin is far from alright.

I stagger away from the circle, drawing the War Mage away from its position. Grant seizes the opportunity and moves next to Ms. Sheldon – where the mage had just been. I stagger away from the circle again, this time causing the killer in the fanged mask to pick up the pace. The Warrior, bewildered and transfixed by his friend's sudden sickness, doesn't even realize he's lowering the axe's blade from Mr. Worthington's throat. With his hostage in tow, he also moves toward me.

The War Mage having moved within an arm's length, I hunch over as though the pain is unbearable and stumble towards the Warrior a mere few feet from me. The ploy works and he relinquishes Mr. Worthington in an effort to catch his wayward soldier. Grant, still in character, runs to Mr. Worthington and pulls him to the other side of the circle, as if guarding him. I've got to admit, I'm already smiling. Alright, actually, that may be a bit of a snarl. Not very lady like, but sometimes I can't help it.

Finding myself in the Warrior's murderous arms, while the War Mage stands over me, I decide it's time to show them where my pain comes from. In a moment, they'll understand it wasn't my appendix bursting or dinosaurs crawling out of my gizzard.

It was Mercy.

I wrestle myself from the Warrior's grasp and spin low to the ground just before he sizzles and rockets away from my suddenly very healthy body. His axe clangs to the floor next to my crouched legs, while his twitching carcass shoots off the opposite direction. Quickly, I turn Mercy toward the War Mage. The person faster than I expected and jumps back to dodge Mercy's tip. I thrust myself upright just in time to counter a slash from the mage's white dagger. The killer tries again, but I'm just fast enough to deflect. This Cronus member is better than Stephen. The mage doesn't just slash at me again without thought. It holds steady, watching me – calculating my next move. We circle one another. The mage places one foot over the other in a graceful ballerina's step. It takes a step forward and I retreat slightly. The fanged killer flicks the dagger toward me, as if about to strike, but stops short in deceit. Unfortunately, I've already lifted Mercy to defend when I notice the feint. Taking advantage of the misdirection, the mage slashes at my undefended mid-section. I leap back just in time for it to catch my robes but little else. The War Mage returns to its defensive state. Due to the shadows created by the blue glowing orb, the killer's eyes are completely absent. Instead, I'm left to look upon two black, hollow pits glaring at me with hellish intent.

As we circle one another, I make sure I'm getting closer to Grant, and the mage is getting further away from him. Just as I'm nearing my teenaged champion, the mage does the most surprising thing. It lunges through the circle, lifting the white blade over its robed head, ready to strike. Matching the movement, I bring up Mercy, ready to defend. But the masked killer does not bring the blade to bear on me. No, with the dagger as high as it can reach, the blade slices through the blue glowing orb causing it to flare in a brilliant blue light as if a thousand flashbulbs going off at once.

Momentarily blinded, I bump into Grant who, of course, accidentally pricks me in the arm with his white dagger. The wound is just enough to make me lose rear back and lose my balance, almost falling on top of him. Grabbing one another, we steady ourselves while we try to regain our eyesight. When I'm finally able to open my eyes, I see an annoying, disjointed white spot in the middle of my vision. But, even with this handicap, I can see the room is filled with darkness. Not a single light source provides any hint of who or what may still be lurking here. The white spot dulling by the second, I fish the flashlight from my pocket. Flicking it on, I shine towards the area where I'd last seen the War Mage.

143

Gone.

Of course it is. I then turn my light toward Grant and Mr. Worthington. I find both still reeling from the light, but no worse for wear. Then, I turn to Ms. Sheldon on the floor – also fine. My nerves still on edge, this is at least a soothing balm.

"Grant," I say, unsure of how safe we truly are, "Untie them."

Finding my mask more debilitating than helpful, I remove it and let it fall to the floor. Grant follows suit and removes his hood just before using his white dagger to cut Mr. Worthington free. While he works, I inch into the darkened corners, letting my flashlight guide the way. I step over the unconscious Warrior and carefully kick his axe toward Grant and the hostages – out of any villain's reach. As I near the office's edge, I hear a rustling to my left. In a split second, my attention beams in the sound's direction as brightly as the flashlight. The next thing I know a single figure is darting right at me – a white dagger in hand. Mercy, with a mind of her own, is already in flight, ready to crash into this person's cranium. I have to pull back as hard as I can to stop the momentum when I see –

"Katie?" I say, trying to stop my single-minded Mercy. Unfortunately, I'm a little too late to stop the momentum completely and Mercy lightly raps the little blonde in the side of the head.

"Ow!' she says, stopping short of hugging me... and probably why she was charging. "Free? Ow..."

"How did you...?" I say so full of relief my mind can't finish a simple sentence.

Attempting to shake away the stars and birds circling her head, she replies, "Crazy War Mage dropped this knife on its way out. I picked it up and cut my ropes... ow..." She cradles the side of her head.

I don't let her hurtful expression last very long. I snatch the girl into my arms, thankful she's unharmed. Holding her there with her father nearby and Ms. Sheldon alive – even if the bad guy got away – I can't think of a happier ending. As if signaling an end to our horrors, the lights in the office flicker on.

"That you, Penny?" I ask, still holding the shaking girl.

My partner in crime might be replying right now. I don't know. I'm too caught up in relinquishing my grip on the girl and watching as she dashes to her father's open arms. They embrace in a hug worthy of greeting cards. The outpouring of emotion is infectious. He cradles her, like a caring father should, happy to see his girl is unharmed. And Katie... she revels in the security of her father's arms. Ms. Sheldon, now untied and standing next to Grant, clasps her hands in relief and joy to see her family safe. Grant, his ever typical self, tries not to intrude, but his puppy dog eyes tell of how truly thrilled he is to see Katie, and how much he too wants to take her in his arms. When the girl notices him standing next to her father, unwilling to call attention to his own heroism, the girl holds out her hand. As she and her dad remain in their embrace, she lovingly takes Grant's hand in gratitude.

I've already heard the army of footsteps echoing from downstairs and glanced over my shoulder to see Dust and the cavalry traversing the main floor. So, I've little to worry about until he arrives. If the War Mage is still in the building, they'll find it. Dust charges through the glass office door with his weapon ready. Three officers – including his partner, Cliff – follow in tow. Noting the family bonding occurring in the middle of the room, he lowers his weapon slightly but does not put it away.

Looking to me he asks with some relief, "You okay?"

I've got to admit, I kind of dig it that he's always worried about me.

"I'm all aces," I reply. "I'm just glad I... *we* got here in time." I say this sincerely, wanting to make sure Grant gets the credit he deserves.

Dust's heart sinks a little when he sees Grant holding Katie's hand and gazing upon her with the biggest fawn eyes this side of Bambi's forest. Turning to Mr. Worthington, the man who has yet to let his little girl go, Dust's relief sinks further. I don't understand why, but the scene makes him incredibly uncomfortable. Something's very wrong.

"Mr. Worthington," Dust says in an attempt to draw his attention. The ploy works and Worthington loosens his grip on his girl without letting go. "Are you okay, sir?"

"Yes," he says to Dust just before gazing into his daughter's pretty eyes. "I am now."

"And you, Ma'am?" he asks Ms. Sheldon.

"Yes," she replies with much heart. "We're all safe now thanks to Free and this fine young man."

Katie squeezes Grant's hand harder as Ms. Sheldon speaks, causing Dust to swallow his discomfort further.

145

"I'm glad to hear it," he replies, removing steel handcuffs from his pocket.

I look over to the Warrior I knocked unconscious, expecting Dust to scoop him up and cuff him, but the other cops have already taken care of him. They're removing his mask to reveal some freckled, red-haired young man who looks about as threatening as Howdy Doody – not the warrior one would expect. So, when Dust walks toward the Worthingtons, his cuffs ready, I couldn't be taken more off guard.

"I'm sorry to do this, sir," Dust begins. "But, Katie Worthington, you are under arrest for conspiracy to commit murder and the murder of Phillip Loughton."

Dust, realizing what this must mean to Grant, carefully removes the boys grip from her hand and snaps a cuff on her. With years of practice, before Mr. Worthington or Katie realize it, he's gingerly removed Katie's other arm from her father and wrestled it behind her to snap on the other cuff.

"Officer!" Mr. Worthington exclaims. "What are you doing?"

"Yeah, Dust!" I call, equally angry and confused. "What the hell?"

"Penny didn't tell you?" he asks. "We've found evidence linking Katie to Cronus Falls."

"Yeah, but..." Grant breaks in, ready to wrestle Dust for Katie, "But we knew that. She quit."

"No," Dust replies, "She didn't. I'll let Penny explain, but, Mr. Worthington, I sincerely apologize – your daughter is under arrest and must come to the station with us."

"What?" Katie cries, her happy, full eyes having turned to shock and horror. "No! I didn't!"

"Katie," Mr. Worthington orders. "Don't you say a word until we have a lawyer."

"But, I didn't!" she cries, tears clouding her pretty eyes.

Dust hands off Katie to Cliff who begins reading her Miranda rights. Mr. Worthington, not believing a word of what is going on, launches into a tirade against my old friend like only a protecting father could. Dust keeps a level head. Receiving such berating on a daily basis, he's become nearly immune. I'm still firmly in awe but manage to throw a consoling arm around Grant. The young man stands with his mouth agape, utterly crestfallen.

"This has got to be a mistake," Grant mutters.

146

FREELANCER

Breaking in, Penny says, "Sorry, Grant. I didn't find out until you guys were in the middle of sneaking into the office. Dust's team found evidence that Katie has been part of Cronus Falls the entire time."

"But we played with her," I interject. "And you checked her online account. She didn't have any more contact with her Cronus friends."

"I checked one account," Penny replies. "Dust's team turned up another hidden account for Katie. It looks like she really did quit playing with Cronus Falls for a long time, but then she came back as a... War God or whatever it's called."

"Warmaster," Grant says, his heart breaking further.

"From the messages Dust found," Penny continues, "It sounds like Katie has been orchestrating all of this."

"This can't be true," Grant mutters. "It's not..."

"I'm sorry, little brother," Penny says with all the heart of an older sister. "But all the evidence points to her."

I watch as Worthington berates Dust further, and Katie is escorted from the office. She turns her eyes to me, looking for some hope – for me to save her. But, I can't. If Dust is right, it sounds like she needed saving long before she ever met me.

147

Chapter 14
A Wizard, a Warrior, and a Killer
Walk into a Bar

Even after Grant and I returned to the apartment, we were still up until 6 a.m. with Penny. Poor Grant was shaken to his core, unable to wrap his mind around any of the events preceding. Penny did her best to console him – to explain how such deceit could occur and how none of it was his fault. Out of character for me, I couldn't say anything. I had nothing to add. Like him, I was torn. Getting fooled by someone comes with the territory when you have my life. If you need proof, remind me to tell you sometime about my ex-boyfriend on death row. But Katie... I just didn't see it in her. Most people, whether they'll admit to it or not, have the capacity to kill. Sadly, there's something ingrained in our DNA which prompts this. It shuts off our conscience just long enough to commit the deed – whether that is in wartime, because our loved ones are in danger, or due to murderous intent depends on the person. But it seems like 99% of all people on Earth have that chromosome. I know I have it. Penny has it. I know for a fact Dust has it... but Katie? I just don't see it in her. Maybe that's why it's 10 a.m. and I'm wide awake again.

Someone is stirring in the bathroom, clanking around the sink. They've already showered and are likely getting ready to start their day. If I had to guess, I'd say it's Grant. I can't imagine he's slept any better than me. Had we not been exhausted after last night, I'm not sure either of us would have slept the few unsettled hours we did. Feeling as though I shouldn't leave him alone and knowing I won't be going back to sleep anytime soon, I toss the covers from me as if they are the cause of my unbalanced dreams. Wearing sweatpants and a ratty Janis Joplin t-shirt – my oh-so-sexy sleepwear when I'm depressed – I roll out of bed and trudge toward the door.

I don't bother to throw on a robe or anything. I'm not exactly the model of sexuality right now and Grant has seen me in this a thousand times. As I exit my bedroom, I can see every door in our hall – the guest room/office, Penny's room, and mine are all open. The only one closed at the moment is the restroom. From the kitchen, I can smell the faint aroma of my caffeinated friend and hear the familiar grunt and slaughter of a certain video game, meaning I was wrong about the restroom's occupant.

As I exit the hall and enter the living room and kitchen beside, I find Grant – hair a mess and the clothes he slept in – playing Fantasy War. He does so alone – none of his online friends invited to this particular session. Looking to my right, I see the lovely, worried eyes of my mother sitting on the opposite side of the bar. Today she's wearing her jogging gear, as if she's headed to the gym after stopping by. What a stark contrast we are. Mom, almost forty years old, looks as pretty and buxom as a pin-up half her age, while her daughter – disheveled and lost – couldn't look homelier.

With nothing but love, Mom asks, "You okay? Grant told me what happened." She slides a full cup of coffee across our bar. That's Mom – still taking care of me.

Taking an aloof seat, I reply lowly, "I'm fine. More worried about him." I nod toward Grant. "Can't believe he's playing that game after everything that happened."

"He says," she begins with her loving grace, "It will help him solve the case. He's using it to think and look for clues."

I let out a sad laugh. It's nice to know our little Grant won't give up on someone he cares about. He's definitely becoming a noble young man. I just wish he didn't also have to learn sometimes you need to let go.

Seeing how depressed her little girl is, Mom lifts a package from the floor. The small parcel, two and half feet long and a foot wide, is white with a deep red bow. She places it in front of me without any real pomp or circumstance.

"I found this waiting at the front door when I arrived," She says with a cocked eyebrow. "Does someone have an admirer I should know about? Or is this a booty call you'll pretend never happened, but Penny will fill me in on later?"

"Mother!" I say more for the fact Grant can hear us. A comment like that, sure, I'm used to from her. Mom's more concerned with my love and/or sex life than I am. She thinks I'm too closed off to the idea of relationships... which I probably am. But she could at least let the girl talk stay between us girls.

I pull the bow's string to untangle the dainty mess of crimson and lift off the present's top. Making my way through a bushel of tissue paper, at first glimpse I spy something red and silky. Then, as I peel through the layers, I find a very well-meaning surprise. There, pristine and perfect, is a little red cocktail dress. Much like the one destroyed just days ago, but much more elegant and – most likely – more expensive than I could ever afford, the dress shimmers with the same gallantry as a wink and nod from a handsome man. Lifting the dress from the box, Mom actually gasps.

"Oh, that is so boddin' gorgeous," she says with my lingo.

"It is absolutely..." I say somewhat in awe before adding, "And stop using my words."

"No need to get amped about it," she says sarcastically.

Ogling the dress and completely unwilling to take my eyes from it, I reply, "See, now you're not even using them right."

Snapping away from the dress, I swim through the tissue paper to find a small card inside. Plain and white, it has something very simple inscribed on it.

ALWAYS LOOK DEEPER.
-Ketchum-

My blushing schoolgirl grin is giving me away.

"So, my girl may really have an admirer?" Mom quizzes with much curiosity.

"No," I reply, putting the card on the stool beside me – purposely away from her prying eyes. "He's just a friend."

"Mmm-hmm..." she's says not buying a word.

I would really like to change the subject now. Explaining Ketchum to her would just be... uncomfortable to say the least. Thankfully, the battle cry coming from our television and mutterings Grant makes as he vanquishes a foe leaves me an opening.

"Feel like that thing is evil," I say to her of Fantasy War. "Feel like all games are evil now. Kids just pervert them into something wrong... or the game perverts kids into something wrong... I can't tell. I'm not awake enough to form a real opinion yet."

"Oh, bullshit, honey," Mom replies with no ill-intent. "Rock-and-Roll is evil. Television is evil. Video games are evil. The internet is evil. I'm not that old yet, but I've still heard'em all. Come on, what's the worst game you played when you were a kid? I mean, so bad you never wanted me to know?" Somewhat ashamed to answer, I take a sip of my coffee in an effort to stave off her question. "And just so we're clear," Mom continues, realizing what I'm doing, "I'm not trying to trap you with this. I just need an example."

My lip jars to the side of my mouth in hesitation. I don't know if I really want to tattle on me and Pen.

"Well," I say hesitantly, "There was this one game Penny and I played all the time that you never knew about. We could actually chainsaw each other in half. It was about the most gruesome thing I'd ever seen... kind of loved it too..."

Mom, unsurprised but still unhappy, replies, "Well... while that doesn't make me feel good about my parenting skills... do you see my point? Are you and Penny going around chainsawing people in half? Did it make you a homicidal person?"

"No," I answer. "But I do beat people up sometimes."

"Well, yeah," Mom says matter-of-fact. "But they deserve it. Plus, you don't dress up in silver and black body armor with LED lights and cut them in two when you do it."

"Body armor with lights?" I ask with some exclamation. "You know the game?"

Mom, unwilling to admit exactly the nature of this knowledge, replies, "I may have known someone a long time ago who... never mind. The point is – It didn't warp you. Just like music and television, our brains try to mimic what we like. It informs the way we dress, how we talk –."

"How we kill people," I interject.

151

Mom, with a shrug, answers, "Yes, but it's not the cause. It's the reflection. A murderous person is going to commit murder regardless of what video game or movie they decide to mimic – just like I'm still going to wear a coat on a cold day. But when I go to buy my coat, I might pick one similar to something I saw on my favorite TV show – something I have a connection with – over a coat I've never seen before. Heck, your next case might be about some starlet who gets murdered by someone dressed like a character from her movie. That's not the movie's fault. The nutbag in the costume is to blame."

"Damn, Jennifer," Penny adds, her slippered feet shuffling into the room. Her body is enveloped in a dark blue robe and her head wrapped in a towel. "You should have been a shrink."

Mom gets a somewhat far off look and forces a laugh, making me think maybe at one time that's what she wanted. But like all great women of compromise, she gave up on that dream when she had me.

"Maybe in another lifetime," she reflects. Letting the statement waft through the air like the coffee in our pot, we don't speak until the odor has cleared.

Breaking the silence, Penny looks to the open box and says, "Oh, I see you finally opened your present. How do you like the dress?" She says this as though she already knew what resided inside.

"How in the hell did you know it was a dress?" I ask.

"When Jennifer used the restroom earlier, I opened it," she says as though my privacy means nothing. "I thought I did a pretty good job re-tying the bow. Anyway, Dust called. Said they've processed..." She stops short of saying Katie's name, knowing it might upset her brother.

"I still don't know if I buy it," I reply lowly. I simply can't rationalize the events of the night before. "Not everything adds up. Katie didn't need to be so close to us. She didn't need to drop by last night or hang out with me yesterday."

"Unless she was building a cover story," Penny contends, walking to the kitchen and fetching a juice glass. "In her warped little mind, maybe she was concocting an alibi. And if she was, it worked." She opens the refrigerator and pours herself a glass of OJ. Wish I could survive the morning on anything other than caffeine.

"Still though," I reply, sipping my coffee, "Seems like she could come up with a better way. Plus, did Dust ever explain that hanging blue orb?"

My robed roommate takes a seat next to Mom and eyes her brother playing Fantasy War on the couch. She, like me, is very worried about him.

"No," Penny replies. "That's the one nagging thing I can't let go of. There's no explanation for it."

"From what you explained, Penny," Mom interjects, "Couldn't it have been some sort of hologram or illusion? Televisions and computers have come a long way."

"Normally," Penny replies, "I'd agree, but this thing actually shattered and flashed when someone hit it. Plus, there was no sign of any device in the rooms where Mr. Loughton was killed or Mr. Worthington's office."

"Well, then," Mom jokes. "I think we have our explanation. It's magic! The wizards you took on were real! Good job, honey!" She let's out a good laugh at the notion and lands a sarcastic hand of congratulations on my own. I snicker as well, but more at her for being so silly than her terrible joke. However, Penny's face glazes over in the most uncomfortable expression, prompting our laughter to abruptly taper off. Mom, noting the look, turns her own uncomfortable expression to the girl and asks, "Wait, it's not magic? Is it?"

"Actually," she begins hesitantly. Penny waves her hand over the bar top, turning on the embedded computer. "There's something I realized about those markings on the knife you first ran into and the symbols on the floors at the crime scenes." She pulls up the 3-D image Grant had created from the white knife that almost killed me. "The symbols Cronus Falls used are real."

Puzzled, I ask, "Define *real*."

"Okay," Penny begins, "They aren't fictional. The reason we couldn't find those symbols anywhere at first was because Fantasy War made them up, or so we thought. The real reason is because those symbols aren't just from Fantasy War. Cronus actually amended them, tweaked the symbols for their own use. If you look at the carvings on the knife carefully, most of them are comprised of two or more symbols. Add a line here and there and suddenly there's a whole new level underneath."

Trying to grasp Pen's meaning, Mom asks, "So they took fake symbols and scratched real ones inside them?"

Penny, not wanting to correct my mother, replies, "Kind of. But, like I said, they more or less added a second symbol using the lines already there."

153

"That's just weird," I put in with my words of wisdom. "So what do they mean?"

"Nothing good," Penny replies. "You've got all kinds of weird black magic stuff laced into these things. Makes me think someone in the guild was trying to hide the fact they were using the group to commit ritualistic killings – and not just some fantasy based crime."

"Ugh," Mom adds with the same eloquence of her daughter. "And I thought the world couldn't get any worse."

"I don't believe in magic," I inform my roommate with a cocked eyebrow. I don't continue, but instead use my disbelieving face to tell her she needs a new theory.

"Sorry, but that's the best explanation I've got," Penny replies. "Until someone comes up with another, you're stuck with it."

Penny replaces the image of the knife with a three dimensional rendering of Katie's Warmaster profile. The character's name, Eliza, and image rotate before us. The fictional character, absent the War Mage's silver fanged mask, is all of five foot three, one hundred pounds, and blond with elf ears. A crazy, pagan tattoo circles her brow and cheek bone. The character's dress is elegant with gold plated War Mage armor with a ruby encrusted center – likely symbolizing the godlike status of the character. The Warmaster, unlike Katie's other character, is practically her spitting image with a few liberties taken.

"So," I begin with some sarcasm, "We have a magic orb, a dead body, and a little blond killer – not really buying any of it."

"Me either!" a cry from the couch insists. Grant, tossing down his controller and finally turning off the game, has obviously been listening the entire time.

"Color me surprised..." Penny says as flip as she can get.

"Grant, sweetie," I say, "None of us want to believe Katie is involved, but she's the most likely suspect at this point." The young man exits his couchly confines and marches to the women folk in the kitchen like he's coming to save the day.

"Yeah, but shouldn't we at least be looking at other suspects?" he points out adamantly. "Just because Katie's the most likely, doesn't make it so."

FREELANCER

Feeling sorry for the boy, my eyes turn from the group and look blankly at the stool next to me. Unfocused and wandering into the void of my subconscious, I don't notice at first the note from Ketchum still lying there. After a moment or two, my eyes regain their focus and stare intently at the words written on the tiny card:

ALWAYS LOOK DEEPER.

My hamster wheel of a brain might need oiling, but it still turns. Unable to piece together where this is taking me, I look curiously to the box housing my new red dress. Tilting my head and sizing up the box, I notice it's a little deeper than the dress I pulled from it. Standing from my seat, I go back to the box and remove the dress. Tossing the incredibly expensive piece of clothing across my shoulder so it is out of my way, I dig both hands into the box and find the cardboard below the dress was actually a false bottom. Peeling back this new layer and dumping the tissue paper on the bar top, I uncover another gift beneath. What I find might not be as expensive and it might not be as fashion sheik, but the meaning is more powerful than anything Ketchum could have purchased. Lifting this new piece of clothing from the box, I can't help smile. A white t-shirt with a red sword – devilish horns protruding from the cross guard and magical energy swirling around the blade – I need no note to tell me what this is:

A Fantasy War t-shirt.

And just like that, Ketchum's words about taking the long way or digging deeper seem to ring true. I might lead us head long into danger, but it's Grant's ever vigilant optimism that's kept us on course. I shouldn't discount him just because I still think of him as a kid.

"Okay then, who is our next suspect?" I ask, my eyes still focused on the t-shirt. "Or are you saying it's just Cronus Falls?"

"In reality," Penny adds, "It's possible the Cronus members are setting Katie up. They hated her, so now they are dragging her down with them."

"Yeah, but," Mom jumps in, "I thought you guys said Tom found messages from her to the killers?" Mom's always called Dust "*Tom*" or "*Thomas*." For some reason it drives me nuts.

"True," Grant adds, "But who says the messages are really from her?"

JEREMY JAYNES

Breaking it down, Penny returns, "I've corroborated the cops' findings... without their knowledge... and Katie really has a second account and sent messages to Cronus members, organizing the killings in various ways. She even organized her own kidnapping."

Mom, unconvinced of any theory, adds, "But why would she kidnap herself? To get away from her Dad? To get away from Free that night? It doesn't add up."

"Don't know," I admit. "But Stephen says he was trying to save her. He could have meant from her dad and us."

"Hold on..." Grant says, as if he's trying to catch an elusive idea forming in his mind. He fans the ember hoping it sparks. "Katie Worthington has an account, right?"

"Yeah," Penny returns, letting her little brother work out whatever is behind his eyes.

"No... no... that's it," he declares, pointing at the Warmaster's image still rotating in front of us. "You don't get it. The name Katie Worthington has an account. Who's to say it's really hers? Free, you and I both know Katie already has a character in Fantasy War – a character she's put a lot of time into, and let's face it, hers looks nothing like this one."

Unsure where this is going, but suspicious, I reply, "Yeah... that Warmaster doesn't seem to be Katie's style. She went out of her way to make her character not look like her. And frankly... I'd expect if she modeled a character after herself, it'd be wearing a lot less clothes."

Penny, with a snort, adds, "That might be the most reasonable assumption I've heard all morning. Still though, that's pretty flimsy."

"Yeah, but when would she have time to create this second character?" Grant questions. "We're talking about a character so powerful it's become the Warmaster – the king daddy of all players in the game. The hours you'd have to put into becoming one is staggering. We're talking three thousand at least. She'd never have enough time to play with both her Barbarian character – who's a higher level than me – and the Warmaster."

"She could have hired someone," Penny contends. "Like a summer job. She could have paid some kid a hundred bucks an hour to level her character up. The girl is rich."

"Forty hours a week," Mom adds, "You could do that over a summer."

I, in my naïve way, ask, "Is that a thing? People pay to do that?"

156

FREELANCER

"Actually, yeah," Mom replies. "I'd heard about it when I was growing up, and I just saw something in the news about it the other day. People who don't have time to play, pay kids to make their characters more powerful. So when they do play, they aren't far behind their friends."

"Thirty points to Jennifer," Penny says with some reward. "Way to go with being hip."

Mom, with the attitude I took from her, says, "I do what I can."

"That's just so…" I have to think about the benefits of this, "Wrong. I mean, games are meant to be fun."

Penny retorts, "Well, yeah, and you're not supposed to dress up like the characters and kill people either. But some people take things too far and ruin it for everyone."

Grant, unwilling to give up, continues, "Okay, I'll concede Katie could have done that… but it's also equally true someone else could have too."

Penny considers her brothers words before relenting, "I can agree with that. And, along those lines, the only thing linking Katie to the Fantasy War account we found was a free e-mail address anyone could register, and the messages were sent from a computer at the public library – meaning anyone could use it. It just happened to have Katie's name on it, and she wrote messages to the other members of Cronus like she was Katie. But, and this is an enormous, overweight-need-to-be-airlifted-from-the-bed-BUTT, how would the other Cronus members not know they had an imposter in their midst? Online I get – you don't see the person – but they would have had to see each other when they committed the murders and realized Katie was struggling when they tried to kidnap her."

This is where I jump in with, "The fanged masks! The person could hide in plain site as long as they are about the same size, don't talk much and/or lower their voice like they did last night. Plus, the club thing, crazy Stephen could have thought her reluctance was all an act for the people watching."

Wow, my brain just spit that out of nowhere.

"Then, if it's not Katie," Grant replies, "Who would have the most to gain by framing her?"

I'm beginning to track where Grant's mind is taking him. New ideas of my own are forming.

157

"The real Warmaster," I say. "The person pulling the strings – the person taking fake symbols and making them real – the person who would need a scapegoat – the one person who would know the difference between fantasy magic and the kind of black magic written about for centuries."

Penny, picking up my threads, hastily taps through the bar computer.

"Yeah, but," Penny begins, disappointed she can't support me, "There aren't any Cronus members who really fit that profile – not perfectly."

"Not Cronus," I reply, a suspect's image fully forming in my mind. "Someone from the group – someone with just as much to lose or gain as Cronus."

My gaze has turned inward and a gloss overwhelmed my eyes. Peripherally, I can see Mom and Grant trade questioning looks, while Penny continues flipping through files on the computer. Hastily, she scans file after file, tossing each aside with the flick of a finger when they do not match. She continues until, suddenly, she pulls her finger away, as if it touched the screen she might erase the evidence before her. Penny's brow crinkles and her mouth opens slightly. Stunning my friend is nigh impossible. Yet, here we are.

I don't let her speak. Instead, I do it for her.

"Only one other person fits the profile," I say with a calm masking my internal storm.

* * *

Waiting in the elegant family room, I adjust the belt on my red coat, ensuring both sides of the leathery strap hang equally. Looking over my wardrobe choice, it really doesn't have much to do with the case. I'm wearing another pair of those spider-webbed jeans – like the ones that introduced me to Beth – a pair of black, flat soled shoes I simply gathered from the floor, and the Fantasy War t-shirt Ketchum left me.

Okay, maybe these items are a bit more symbolic than I thought.

FREELANCER

Knowing my presence has been noted by the invited guest of honor, I'm not nervous. I'm too angry to be nervous. Turning to the pictures of the brunette girl, just out of reach from her father in the family photos, I see that fake smile, lovingly crafted in acting classes to fool others. I also note the photo of the same girl at dance recital – one foot over the other – ever so graceful. I move on to the bookcase next to me full of texts on Theology, the Occult, and murder mysteries. Her father was quiet the collector – seems his daughter picked up where Daddy left off. Taking a step, I accidentally kick a small, cardboard package on the floor. I look down to find the unopened copy of Fantasy War: War Mage Edition – a pricey purchase for someone to never use... not by themselves anyway.

"Free," the dark haired girl calls as she enters the room. With so much heart you'd suspect it to be real, she asks, "I didn't expect you today. I heard about Katie. Is she alright? And, more importantly, are you alright?"

Turning to face her, I suppress my anger and reply, "I'm fine, actually. Thanks for asking, Beth." Adding fuel to the fire I intend to set, I continue, "In fact, Katie's fine too – just got released about an hour ago."

"Oh," Beth says, keeping her calm admirably well. "But I thought she was in jail. Did they release her on bail or something?"

"No," I say, strolling to one of her father's photos on the mantel. "Actually, some new evidence showed up – cleared her right away."

Beth, taking a step toward me, says with Oscar caliber relief, "Well, thank goodness. That's if – that's if they're sure. I don't want the girl in prison, but I still don't trust her if you know what I mean?"

Lifting her father's photo from its perch I examine it closely, practically cradling it with affection. I have no love for this man – never knew him. And if he was as abusive as he seemed, then I'm not even sad to see he's gone. No, I'm simply doing this for reaction. My back is fully turned Beth's way, but I angle the reflection on the frame's glass just enough that I can see her face. Her eyes are full of venom and a dark cloud fills her cheeks as I show faux affection toward this detestable individual.

"Oh, I know what you mean," I say with a hint of sparring. "Um, by the way, do you know someone by the name of Enos Reddings?" I move to another photo and embrace it similarly.

Doing her best to keep the façade, Beth replies, "No, should I? Free, what's this about?"

159

"It's about," I say, returning the picture to the mantel, "A girl who paid Mr. Reddings to play a game for her. A game called Fantasy War."

A crack forms in her armor as she replies, "I don't understand."

"Beth, sweetie, I think ya do," I flippantly reply. Pacing the room, I explain, "You see, this girl – the same one who paid Mr. Reddings – had a lot of trouble at home. Dad was an abusive prick that made her life miserable. The only thing this girl had going for her was this group at school full of similar kids. And one of those kids in particular – Katie – really helped to keep her going. But one day, Katie makes all nice with her dad who – let's face it – was not nearly the bastard this girl's dad was."

Beth's face is growing darker by the second. Oddly, the weather outside seems to mirror the clouds forming in the room and the sun takes refuge behind an ominous stormy sky.

"But as the sessions wore on, she noticed other people in the group also felt betrayed by Katie because – well, honestly – misery loves company. And with Katie's new sunny disposition because her life was better than everyone else's, it just made them feel worse. And that kind of hatred – that's like Ebola. It spreads. It festers – especially if there's some significant abuse going on too."

I turn to a photo of Beth's father and let the comment linger.

"So, the girl, believing her life would never be as good as Katie's, hatched a plan. It started out simple enough. As soon as she sees Katie's no longer friends with her gamer buddies, she makes a fake Fantasy War account under her ex-friend's name. At first, the girl – as Katie – pretends she's trying to win back her friendship with Cronus Falls – some of the kids from the group – but most of the guild isn't into it. To sweeten the pot, she begins telling them things with her dad have gotten worse, and she doesn't see any way out. Some of the Cronus members start voicing similar feelings of hopelessness, but the rest of the group – they aren't ready to take Katie back yet."

Marching to the Fantasy War box on the floor, I pick it up and keep speaking. The clouds outside crackle and pop as if Cronus himself has taken notice of the blasphemy in his name.

"So, to sweeten the pot, the girl enlists this kid, Enos Reddings, to play Fantasy War non-stop. Suddenly, Katie's coming back to Cronus with this uber-powerful War God – or whatever it's called – willing to pledge allegiance to the group. They welcome her back with open arms... and that's where the real manipulation starts. Within a week, Katie and Stephen are talking about all these cryptic things – some of it to do with black magic and empowering the soul – things this girl knows about because her father is an expert in the field. And this all happens, coincidentally, right before Stephen's parents die. Whether she had anything to do with their deaths or not, she uses it to convince others she has power. Of course, once some of the more sane-minded kids start getting suspicious, half the Cronus members quit the group. The girl, the master manipulator she is, even convinces the nutjobs who stick around that they can never meet or call one another for fear they would be discovered. Even if they ran into each other in public, they had to keep their cover. Cronus Falls, to the outside world, couldn't exist anymore. The only time they could officially be in the same place at the same time was when they were in full costume and during a ritual. Oh, and my favorite part is, she probably never intended on killing the other kids' parents. She actually needed Mr. Worthington dead to implicate Katie, but her goal was her own father. And once he and Worthington were dead, well, she'd have no more use for the group. After that... well, you would probably know better than me. Wouldn't you, Beth?"

"Me?" Beth feigns, bewildered by the accusation. "You think I had something to do with this?"

"No, Beth," I reply matter of fact. "I know you had *everything* to do with this."

"I don't know what you're smoking," Beth defends, disgusted at the accusation. "I have absolutely no reason to send myself vials of blood or kill Katie's father."

"Sure you do," I reply without hesitation. "But – and this really is the most ingenious part – you didn't do it. You had your cronies do it. They were out to save Katie and you – just like they said. They sent the vials and the pictures. They even perpetrated your – air quotes – *abduction.* They probably even killed your dad for you."

"I don't know where you get your delusions," Beth replies with a great deal of hostility. "But I'm sure there's no proof of any of this."

"Oh, you think so, do you?" I ask with so much attitude my hips may sway off as I march to her. "You weren't as clever as you thought. You paid Reddings in cash, which was smart, and the only reason we caught him was because he wanted some fancy armor in the game – armor you have to buy. Enos, having no idea he was a patsy in some murder scheme, broke out his own credit card – under the fake Katie's account – and bought it for your War God. Once we had him... well, all it took was one more receipt."

Beth's face erodes into a snarl and a clap of thunder echoes from outside.

"You see because of piracy issues, these days all computer software – video games included – comes with a store-bought authorization code," I explain with some relish. "And you – not being familiar with video games – didn't realize as soon you swiped your credit card for that game, Sensation Limited knew who you were, where you purchased it, and where it was played since that day forward."

Stopping to bask in Beth's dire reflection, I realize something funny.

"So, I guess in a way," I say literally with my tongue in cheek, "The man you tried to murder last night – the last bit to frame Katie – he's the guy who brought you down."

Beth's pretty face has twisted into something exceedingly ugly. Her once lovely eyes are filled with bile and her strong will replaced by murderous intent.

Ignoring her, I add, "So far, the only thing I can't figure out is that damn blue glowing orb. You wanna help me out and explain that? I'm seriously going to lose sleep over it."

Beth, not swayed by my attempt at humor, looks as if she's going to pick up the nearest sharp object and impale me with it. Knowing she very well could, I reach into my coat and take out Mercy. I stop short of whipping it out and showing her I'm ready to go anytime she is. Instead, I just keep her in my hands and make sure Beth knows I'm not defenseless.

FREELANCER

"Do you even know who or what you're dealing with little girl?" Beth spits like some demon seed from a bad movie. "My father may have been a bastard, deserving of roasting on Satan's pike, but he did teach me a great many things. Things you cannot possibly imagine! That orb was just a small taste of the power I wield. And when it comes to full fruition, I will bring all my might down upon you. You could have been my friend, but now you'll be just another bloody footprint under my heel."

As if leaves stirred by a hellish wind, she snatches a glass vase from a nearby end table and charges me. With a flick of a button, Mercy telescopes open. Watching the crazed girl charge, I can only say exactly what I'm thinking.

"Oh, bitch, you are just one big glowing orb of crazy."

As suddenly as the thunder outside, the room reverberates, shaking with such intensity the pictures of Beth's family fall from the mantel. The murderous books on theology and mystery are next to plummet from their shelves, and an iron fireplace poker clangs to the floor. Anger keeps my footing sure while my stance hardly waivers. Beth does her best to match me but sways some in the passing quake. Her unbalanced charge is just enough to ensure my advantage. The vase, over her head and ready to crash down, is no threat to me. With Mercy in hand, I have twice the reach she does. But, this being a special occasion and all, I'm not going to tase her – not just yet anyway. With a snap of my arm, Mercy crashes into the side of Beth's face. The girl's momentum, instead of being stopped, sends her staggering to the right and crashing into a still vibrating lush chair. Pretty sure that's going to leave a mark. The vase plummets to the ground and shatters, mirroring Beth's very sanity. Holding the side of her face, the girl turns a glare upon me which says I'll eat your very soul.

Go for it, sister.

Beth launches from the chair, but the sad, psychotic girl only gets within a few feet of me when I crack her across the skull with Mercy one more time. She staggers and crashes into the shaking mantel beside us. Holding the shelf to keep upright, the girl notes one of her dance trophies – one with a nice pointy star at the top – and reaches for the would-be weapon.

Now, I've had just about enough.

163

JEREMY JAYNES

I smack Mercy across her arm as if it's the nose of a disobedient puppy. Her appendage rears back, but her crazed eyes tell me this only stalls her. In another swift movement, I bring Mercy low and crack the back of Beth's leg, right at the bend of her knee. Her grip on the shaking mantel wanes and she plummets to the floor. As the earthquake subsides, and the room's vibration tapers to an end, the girl, make-up smeared and chin quivering in anger, relents her tears of regret and defeat.

"You think you've got me all figured out," Beth chuckles with watery eyes. She rocks on the floor like a deflated child after her tantrum did not win her way. "You think I'm some crazy rich girl with daddy issues. But the sad part is: Who are you to judge me for pretending to be someone else? You're the girl who dresses in parts and plays a role on a day to day basis? So, what gives you any right to judge me? Who do you think you are?"

In a way, her sick, delusional words hit home. She's right. Who am I to judge someone for pretending to be what they aren't? I don't even know who I am half the time. My head sinks and I look to the red faux leather coat I'm wearing. The red threads are finely woven, with a few frays here and there. The leathery material, stronger than actual animal hide, is probably some sort of plastic simply imitating something weaker than what it truly is. Turning to the Fantasy War t-shirt, I look over the heroic sword and the dangerous bolts of magic swirly around it, while the crossguard's devilish shape proves a match for any foe. I then turn to my slightly provocative jeans, ripped and torn as if they've been through the ringer. They declare their sex appeal without apology, yet are no more risqué in my eyes than a down sweater. And, for once, I tossed these items together not because of the person I thought they would make me, but because of the person I am.

"Beth, who you are is more than the jacket you slide on or the name you write on a check," I reply with some scholarly intent. "It's what's deep down inside us that makes us the people we are. And deep down, you are a wounded girl who chose to manipulate others into doing something black and dark – something that has stained the person you used to be."

"Oh, yeah?" she asks, her psyche breaking down further. "Then, who are you with all your crazy clothes and fake personas?"

164

FREELANCER

The booted heels of Dust and his men are thudding down the hall, so I've little time left with my dear friend on the floor. Soon, they will escort her from here in handcuffs and take her to prison. She may get off. She may not even do time. That's for the lawyers. But her name – her life – will be ruined just like those she manipulated.

Funny thing, with all these thoughts in mind, I probably shouldn't grin while standing over a shaking enemy, but I can't help it. As if a veil has finally been lifted, as if Ketchum's words about looking deeper applied to more than the case, as if everything has taken on a shiny new clarity, my answer becomes so apparently clear.

"Who am I?" I reply with the wit of my mother and the devilish grin granted to me by my father. "I'm Free."

165

<u>Final Case Notes</u>
Penny for your Thoughts

If I had a job description, it would be something like: Give Free the best, most accurate information I have available, while keeping her safe and undistracted by neglecting false, misleading, or half-assed research. Okay, maybe I wouldn't word it like that on a resume, but the fact remains – my job is to give my friend the best tools to do her job, but hold back when needed.

But don't take that the wrong way. I normally don't keep things from Free. If I find something she needs to know about, the only reason I ever hold onto it is to keep her safe or undistracted.

I'm not sure which this falls under. Will this keep her safe? Or will it just distract her?

I tap my pen on the bar top to the rhythm of my own anxiety. Looking at the computer and the files displayed on it, for a split second I consider deleting them – pretending they never existed. But that would be a cheat, and I'd know what I saw.

When I began my little search, it was out of sheer curiosity, and Free's always supported me poking into her family's past. But will she like this? Is this good news or bad?

I hear the jingle of keys at the door and realize I may have to make a decision sooner than I'd like. Instead of closing the page and powering down the bar top computer, I leave it open and available. Now I'm just daring her to look – to see for herself what I found. Then it's done.

Free enters the apartment, red coat and Fantasy War t-shirt still on. She looks tired – exhausted – but somehow happy. I think it went well.

"Did you get her?" I ask.

Free, turning to me with those big brown eyes of hers, advises, "You bet my sweet ass we did!"

FREELANCER

The case is closed and the bad guys – er, girl in this case – is caught. She's positively exuberant... which royally sucks because now might be the best time to lay this on her. Better she's in a good mood when she hears it than bad.

"So, where's Grant?" she asks.

"Oh, you are going to love this," I reply, thankful to change from the subject my mind lingers on. "Little Miss Katie – now free and clear thanks to Team Freelancer..." I trail off pondering how obscenely hokey that name is.

Free, feeling the same way, adds, "Can we not use that name?"

"Absolutely," I agree before continuing, "Katie decided to take him to the movies again today."

"Aw," Free fawns. "Our little Grant has a girlfriend!"

Free makes me feel like such a horrible older sister because I do not gush over him like that.

Bitch.

No, I'm just kidding. I love her. Maybe it's that same thing with adults and other people's kids. You don't have to live with them so of course you consider them little precious angels.

"I wouldn't go so far as *girlfriend*," I reply.

Free, tossing her purse on the bar and slipping off her coat, counters, "You still don't like the girl, do you?"

"It's not that," I admit. "The little tramp grows on you in small doses. I just don't think she likes him that way. She is, after all, a whole year older than him and just graduated high school."

Free, still rooting for the home team, argues, "But a year's not a big deal."

"Oh, you forget," I reply. "This is a sixteen year old girl hanging out with a fifteen year old boy."

Once you get out of high school, age differences really aren't a big deal. But when you're a teenage girl and a younger man is showing interest, well that could be considered ghastly. The disappointed glint in Free's eye tells me she's with me on this.

"Crap," she says in disappointment. "He might as well be twelve."

"Yup," I reply succinctly.

"Well," Free returns with a hint of optimism, "I'm still going to hope for the best. You never know."

167

Taking her coat in hand, she exits the kitchen and crosses into the hallway, headed off to her bedroom. Aggravated, I take my finger and literally spin the ominous file like some virtual square merry-go-round, wishing she'd simply taken an interest before exiting. Damn it, Free. Don't you know you're supposed to look at it and take all the decision making out of the equation?

I skim the file one more time before making any sort of final judgment. Honestly, I was just poking around because of the things Jenny said this morning. She is such a cool mom and she never talks about Free's dad. So, when I get the chance – and again, Free completely knows I dig around like this – I go looking for information on either of them. Well, I didn't expect to find some outdated online storage service with Mr. Freeman's name on it. Hell, Freeman is such a common name, I wasn't even sure it was his. So, when I got into the file... I mentioned it was outdated, right? How little security this online storage service provides is way more criminal than how I got in. Anyway, when I started reading this stuff, I had to do a double take. I thought I was mistaken that maybe somehow I was reading old files from Free. But no, there it was in bold letters on the Business Certificate:

MICHAEL FREEMAN
FREEMAN INVESTIGATIONS

Free's mom had not once mentioned Mr. Freeman was a detective. From the dates on the certificates and his notes, it doesn't look like his career lasted long. He was killed in the quake within a couple years of opening his business. Crazier still, I start looking through his case files and come across his very first client. Mr. Freeman was the cryptic sort, and he only used single names but I don't believe in coincidence, especially when my best friend was born a couple years later. Any bets on the name of his client?

"Jennifer."

But this kind of news? Hell, I'm ready to bust into Free's room with it right now. She'd go nuts – in a good way – to find this out. She'll be pissed at Jennifer to no end – and I can't blame her – but she'll also be ecstatic to know she's walking in her father's shoes. It also explains why Jennifer didn't go completely ballistic when Free started Freelancing. But, as I read further into the file, and more into his cryptic notes, things get a bit fuzzy. In fact, his later notes are written in some sort of shorthand I can't decipher and others have passwords and an encryption that's... well, better than the website they're stored on that's for sure. I'll break them eventually, but I've got to decide what to do with the information I have first.

Heck, these files shouldn't even be here. In fact, this online storage site should have purged these a long time ago, but strange thing is I'm not the only one who's accessed this account in the past year. Someone else has been in here, and they're the reason the files still exist at all. And the kicker? The thing stopping me from telling Free everything I've found just before we jump up and down on her bed like little girls? Okay, actually, for the record we would not do that. Free might, but I'd just stand there and tell her she looks ridiculous.

No, the thing stopping me is one name – one name attached to Mr. Freeman's first case that doesn't make sense. He'd be like a teenager – Grant's age – when this case was going on, so I don't know how it's possible. It has to be a coincidence... but, damn it... like I said, I don't believe in coincidence. But I also don't give Free half-assed information that might hurt more than help.

"Penny," Free calls from her bedroom. "You wanna come talk for a bit."

Letting out a huffy breath, I should have expected this. After a hard case – and this has truly been the hardest, no matter what Free says – she always sleeps the next day away. But before she can, she needs me to talk her down, wear off the adrenaline, while she drifts into unconsciousness. Call it our ritual if you want. Regardless, I now have no choice. Until I have real facts, I may need to omit our mysterious caller's name... for now... but the rest she should know.

"Coming, Free," I call from the kitchen. Loading the file to my glass tablet, I hop from the table. "There's something I wanted to tell you anyway."

169

JEREMY JAYNES

I'm betting this is not going to help her sleep, but she needs to know. I'll just leave out that pesky name confusing the heck out of me though – at least until I have more information. I mean, what are the odds anyway? So, in an effort to protect my friend, I'll simply show her the rest of the file and omit that one detail keeping her from losing further sleep. Looking at the page one last time as I walk down the hall, I glare with a weightless heart upon the name just before highlighting and encrypting a single word:

KETCHUM

Jeremy Jaynes is author of The Golden Kingdom series and a graduate of Ball State University where he obtained a degree in Professional English with a focus on Professional Writing. He was born and raised in Seymour, Indiana where many of his friends and family still live.

He currently lives with his wife in Indianapolis, while working on further projects, including following entries in The Golden Kingdom and Freelancer series.

You may read more about Jaynes' work at:
www.PhoenixOneAlpha.com

Or, follow him on Twitter at:
twitter.com/JeremyJaynes

If you liked *Freelancer*, look out for:

 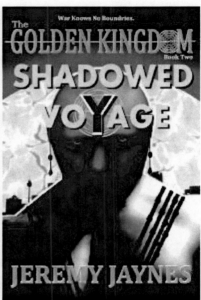

Also from Jeremy Jaynes and Phoenix One Media!

www.PhoenixOneAlpha.com

CPSIA information can be obtained at www.ICGtesting.com
Printed in the USA
LVOW061504300612

288338LV00001B/7/P